DINNER *with* ELOÏSE

ALSO BY COUNT COLLIN VAN REENAN

The Spaces in Between

DINNER
with
ELOÏSE

COUNT COLLIN VAN REENAN

Red Door

Published by RedDoor
www.reddoorpress.co.uk

ISBN 978-1-913062-96-5

A CIP catalogue record for this book is available from the British
Library

Cover design: Patrick Knowles

Typesetting: Jen Parker, Fuzzy Flamingo
www.fuzzyflamingo.co.uk

Printed and bound in the UK by CPI Group (UK), Croydon

For Wendy

'I have love in me the likes of which you can scarcely imagine and rage the likes of which you would not believe. If I cannot satisfy the one, I will indulge the other.'

MARY SHELLEY, *FRANKENSTEIN*

CHAPTER 1

Darkness is a lonely place.

*Y*ou can't have it both ways; you can't have the fantasy *and* the reality. I always sleep face down. If I can sleep at all. When your head is in the pillow, you don't know if it's morning because it still seems dark. But this morning I woke up on my back and saw the sunlight streaming in from a crack in the curtains, making bright bars across the duvet.

My bedroom, like all the rooms in the cottage, was tiny with a low, beamed ceiling and a small bay window of real leaded glass. In spite of the curtains, the room was full of light and I took that to be a good omen for my first day there. It was only a few steps to the tiny bathroom and even smaller kitchen, which was really a lean-to stuck on the garden side of the place. Being just over six feet, I had to duck down but I still managed to hit my head on at least two of the beams. Coffee in hand and slumped in the battered leather chair that was, so far, the only decent piece of furniture in my sitting room, I considered my first important decision since moving in: should I keep taking the medication or should I start my new life free of any chemical influence? I examined the aluminium foil packs, with their tablets in blisters, looking like sweets but having such a devastating effect on me since the first day they were prescribed. When I told that to my psychiatrist, her reply was to ask me how I thought I would feel *without* them. I mean, what sort of question is that? Psychiatrists can be very smug; they think their concepts of reality actually exist.

Finally, I opened a drawer in my desk, threw the whole lot inside, slammed it shut and, feeling that I'd struck a small blow at the tyranny of depressive illness, made some more coffee and walked with it out into the back garden.

For a tiny cottage, the garden seemed vast. Its complicated and artistic layout must have once been a local wonder but years of neglect had rendered it little short of a wilderness.

The morning felt fresh and clean and countrified and I sat on the back doorstep trying to decide which way to tackle the jumbled mess of shrubs. It was so quiet.

'Mr Jack!' a strident voice called just behind me and I heard Lorca's footfall on the stone slabs of the kitchen floor.

'Mr Jack – sitting in the sun – that's nice. How was your sleeping this first night? Good, I hope. Nice and tight.'

Lorca's grasp of the English language was not that great and she had particular problems with idioms. After helping me move in the previous day, she had gone off to her lodgings wishing me to 'sleep tightly'.

Her head and shoulders appeared behind me over the bottom half of the stable-type back door, squinting into the bright sunlight. Tall and slim, with longish brown hair and hazel eyes, she was really quite good looking. Watching her open the bottom half of the door, I realised that I knew little else about her – whether she was married or had kids. If she did, she had left them back in Romania. My friends, the ones who had cared for me since the 'Event', had found this place for me when I was discharged from the sanatorium and had sorted everything out. They had to because they held power of attorney over all my affairs. Apparently, there was enough money left from the sale of the London flat to buy this cottage outright, give me a small monthly allowance and pay Lorca's wages. She was a sort of housekeeper but she didn't live in and was supposed to come four days each week to do my washing, some cooking and generally keep an eye on me. I don't know to what extent she was actually supposed to be my carer but she was. It started with her fussing around me during the moving in and she all but tucked me up in bed the first night. Now she was doing it again, scrutinising me, how I was dressed, whether I'd combed my hair or cut myself shaving. I didn't mind; there was nobody else to take an interest. I had long since realised that I could control nothing of importance that happened to me.

'I make some coffee, Mr Jack.' I couldn't tell whether it was a statement or a question, her accent was so strong. 'Now, did you take medication yet?'

'Yes, earlier this morning,' I lied, half afraid she might check the plastic tablet holder thing. To avoid any more questions, I got busy measuring the garden.

I was very isolated here. The cottage had no near neighbours and very little traffic used the narrow lane save for the occasional tractor and a few horses. About two miles down the lane, westbound, was apparently a village comprised of a public house, a butcher's and a post office that sold groceries. If that wasn't luxury enough, the cottage had electricity and mains water.

In the kitchen, I heard Lorca talking to herself as she tinkered with the washing machine and by the time she had put on a wash and made coffee, I was back indoors drawing up plans for my garden.

Lorca took an interest in everything I did and I suppose I should have been grateful that she was concerned about me but it's a very blurred line between inquisitive and nosy. She had a disconcerting habit of staring at me while I was answering her questions, as if she were looking for signs of deception on my part and, it seemed to me, treated some of my replies with obvious scepticism.

Lorca went about mid-afternoon and left me some dinner. I read into the evening and, physically tired from manual labour in the garden, I went to bed early and for the first time in many months slept the whole night without a nightmare. It was the same thing the next night but by day three I was beginning to feel restless.

The wine, beer and champagne my friends had bought for the moving-in party had all gone. It was one of Lorca's days off.

Though I had been looking forward to isolation, the novelty had worn off a bit and I felt in need of chatting to someone or at least seeing some people. One of the benefits of stopping the medication was the pleasure of being able to drink alcohol again and working outside gave me a real thirst. So it seemed like a good time to explore and find the local village and its pub.

Opposite the tall hedge of my cottage fronting the narrow lane was a large area of woodland with a broad path leading into it, more or less in front of my gate. I wandered in and was immediately entranced by the sudden change to the forest at its best, with carpets of bluebells and primroses backed by a mixture of different deciduous trees like a scene from a chocolate box lid.

After about ten minutes on the narrowing grassy track, heading, as far as I could tell by the sun, due west, I came out onto a hard road that I guessed was the same lane that ran past my cottage but lower down the hill that led to the village. It took me at least half an hour to walk back up the lane to my cottage so a stroll through the beautiful wood took at least a mile off the walk to the village. During all this time I saw no one and only a couple of cars; until then I hadn't realised how isolated this place was.

Early evening saw me out again and this time following the lane towards the village. The going was mainly downhill and I soon passed the junction with the woodland path. There were now houses either side of the lane but they were few and far between with tall thickets filling the spaces. It was so quiet. Nobody was about, even in the gardens. Eventually, the frequency of the houses increased and I passed a crossroad with a shop, post office, telephone box and wooden bus shelter.

I had been told by the estate agent that there was a pub, so continued, slightly uphill, past allotments, a farm and a few big houses with long drives, until I could make out an old, timber-framed, white-boarded building hung with flower baskets and a faded sign with a horse's head.

It was a warm spring evening and the smell of beer on the cool air coming from the open door drove me on. The interior seemed dark after the brash sunshine and the low ceiling beams meant that I had to duck my head here and there until I reached the old mahogany bar with its polished copper top where my eyes were drawn to the ebony and brass beer pumps.

An attractive short-haired girl appeared behind them and asked the question.

'Guinness, please.' I forced myself to smile at her. She was the only person other than Lorca that I had seen in a week. She smiled back and we both stared patiently at the glass as the foam began to settle. As I paid, I was tempted to start a conversation with her but the place was busy and she seemed to be the only barmaid. Carefully carrying my pint, I moved further into the L-shaped room and out through the open French doors to the tables in the beer garden.

As I did so, I passed a pretty girl with very long blonde hair quite elaborately plaited and styled in a way reminiscent of pictures I had seen of young Red Indian girls. She wore a long white summer dress but, somewhat incongruously, she was rolling a cigarette using liquorice paper and sprinkling a suspicious looking dark substance into the tobacco already in place.

She looked up suddenly, caught me looking at her, smiled and said, 'Hello. You're new here, aren't you?'

I really didn't want to talk but didn't want to be rude either so I just hovered next to her and we exchanged names and tried awkwardly to shake hands while I held my beer and she balanced her roll-up. After that, I made an excuse to wander back inside. I detest smoking and find the smell of pot very unpleasant. Back in the bar area, things had livened up judging by their nods in my direction. Apparently, it was music night and they appeared to think I was one of a group of people who followed the various bands.

After a lengthy tuning up and much one–two, one–two testing of the microphones, the band started well and it was wonderful to be listening to live music, surrounded by people who seemed intent on having a good time.

Back in the late sixties as a student in Paris, I loved to go from bar to bar listening to the various bands. Paris was full of music in those days, not like now, when a licence is required to even play a radio in a café.

After so much isolation, the music, the company and especially the beer were like a return to long ago happier times. No longer restricted by medication, I over-indulged, and by the time I left, it was very late and the effect of the beer weighed heavily on me. It was very dark, with a new moon and just the stars offering a glimmer of light. I was swaying around a bit but there was no traffic and I reasoned that I couldn't get lost if I just followed the road.

The first few hundred yards were pleasant enough but as the

distance from the pub increased my feeling of euphoria wore off and I began to realise that I had a long walk ahead of me and should have gone easier on the beer, especially after such a long abstinence. It was very dark now and only the occasional street lamp lit the way. Here and there, the cottages showing lighted windows were too far back from the road to shed any useful light on the lane.

After about ten minutes of unsteady walking, I came to the centre of the village with its T-junction, bus shelter and war memorial. Here, there was a zebra crossing with orange light from the flashing beacons giving the surrounding area a more cheerful look, but within a few minutes of leaving this central area behind me, I was plunged back into darkness. To add to my rising uneasiness, the few street lamps suddenly went out and I guessed it was midnight.

It is a shameful fact that, well-built and fit as I am, I have always been afraid of the dark. Perhaps it stems from my childhood in the countryside when we had oil lamps and candles and had to use torches when we went out at night, and maybe later, when I lived in London and in Paris, I became used to the street and shop lights being on all the time. Whatever the reason, I now felt uncomfortable and that made my next decision all the more incredible.

Intoxication was probably to blame but whatever blurred my decision-making, I decided to take the woodland path that I had discovered earlier that day. I suppose I must have reasoned that it would cut twenty minutes off my journey and that the woods could be no darker than the lane. I was wrong on both counts.

The initial twenty or thirty yards inside the wood were not too bad. The path was quite wide and just discernible in the faint light coming from the stars. But then things began to change rapidly. Suddenly the path became narrower and swung to the left, closing the ingress of starlight; the trees that had been large and widely spaced became more numerous and closer together until they closed into a canopy overhead, shutting off completely the weak light from the sky.

Before I really registered it, I found that I was in pitch darkness. Had I turned back then, I might well have been able to retrace my steps but instead I blundered forwards, arms automatically outstretched. Within minutes, I was in deep trouble, unable to see anything at all in front of me. Then I was on the ground, having tripped over something, perhaps a root or fallen branch that lay directly in my path. The fall winded me but I seemed unhurt. Scrambling up, I realised with dismay that I no longer knew which way I had been facing. I'd had some vague notion of just keeping on straight ahead, believing that I must be closer to the cottage side of the wood but now I had no idea which direction I was walking in – if it could be described as walking. In fact, I was just edging forward very slowly, arms held out in front of me like a stage sleepwalker. My hands touched what must have been slimy bark and then dew-damp leaves slithered across my face. Panicking now, I was sobering up very fast, aware of the precarious situation I was in. I stopped moving and forced my brain to think. It seemed obvious that I could stumble about in the blackness all night and the possibility of finding the way out by chance was remote. More likely I would be crashing into a tree or hitting my head on a branch. I felt completely sober now and tried to think of a solution. If I kept on trying to walk, I would stumble around directionless and would eventually injure myself. The only sensible thing to do was to find a large tree trunk and sit down with my back against it and wait for it to get lighter. I reckoned that, at that time of year, dawn would be only three to four hours away and perhaps I could sleep most of that.

By very cautiously groping about, I soon found what must

have been a very large tree – probably one of the oaks that I'd noticed earlier in the day. It was coarse and a bit slimy from heavy dew that was settling and dampening the shoulders of my jacket and now that I was no longer moving, I began to feel the chill.

It was pitch black all around me and at first seemed totally silent. The only thing that I was aware of was the hard, uneven tree trunk at my back. Laying my now aching head on my drawn-up knees, I tried to sleep. It was only then that I noticed that what I had taken for total silence was anything but quiet.

Slowly at first, then gradually, I became aware of a variety of sounds. At first, it was a slight scurrying sound that I imagined must be some small creature moving stealthily over the fallen leaves then, startling me, the sharp cracking of a twig followed by the loud snapping of a stick. Immediately, I thought that someone was coming through the woods and looked around for signs of torchlight. Nothing, however, penetrated the blackness. So what was heavy enough to break a stick so loudly and make apparently swift progress in total darkness without a torch? I tried to get a grip on my nerves by thinking logically: there were no predators in England capable of hunting a human, and the biggest animal in that wood could only be a fox or a badger. But could a fox snap a thick stick? And, anyway, would it approach when its sense of smell would tell it of a human presence?

Suddenly, there was another noise that sounded like a sniff, then another and another, closer every time, accompanied by a strange, musky smell.

I was now seriously rattled and my whole body cringed as though anticipating an attack. I began to believe that I was surrounded by weird creatures standing just inches away in the darkness.

Desperate to get a grip on my totally illogical fears, I told myself that I was being stupid and childish to panic. With my back pressed hard against the tree trunk and my knees drawn up to my chest, I fought to control my fear of the darkness but it was welling up from some deep, primordial instinct passed down from our ancestors who had good reason to fear the dark. Imagination was my worst enemy and I fought it with my eyes closed and my head tucked in with my hands over my ears. Ridiculous: at six foot one I was a match for even a human attacker. Even so, my body cringed in expectation of being touched by some spectral hand or of some ghostly, cold face pressing my cheek.

I suppose even fear has its limits and it was slowly and imperceptibly replaced by exhaustion. Somehow, I must have slept because when I opened my eyes, the darkness had been replaced by a grey mist. It swirled around the ground at the foot of the trees so that when I stood up out of it, stiff and chilled to the bone, I could see quite clearly where I was – just a few yards from the broad track that led through the woods! Whichever direction I now took, I knew that it would bring me out onto the lane and it so happened that I chose the direction that brought me out in front of my cottage.

Mercifully, Lorca wasn't due to work that day and I was able to take a bath to warm up and go straight to bed.

I don't know why I was so concerned about Lorca's opinion but I just knew that she would disapprove, give me a lecture about drinking and ask me whether I was taking my medication. She seemed more like my minder than my cleaner and perhaps I should have called her 'Auntie' Lorca.

CHAPTER 2

*'Who are you? Why do you hide in the darkness and
listen to my private thoughts?'*
WILLIAM SHAKESPEARE, *ROMEO AND JULIET*

I decided to forego the gardening the next day. Instead, I walked three miles into the nearest small town with a library and looked up 'night vision' in their encyclopaedia. From what I read, it seemed that improving night vision was mainly a question of good eye health, vitamin A and a few simple tricks such as opening your eyes very wide to take in a maximum of light and squeezing them shut for ten seconds before looking into the dark. Always a bit of a sceptic, the only thing I felt able to accept was the avoidance of very bright lights. By gradually diminishing a light source, the eyes will become accustomed to it and the pupils open wider to give the retina the maximum amount of light available.

Armed with this information and a determination to put it into practice, I returned to the cottage and made straight for the small barn that acted both as a garden shed and as a garage, should I ever have a car. I remembered a smell of paraffin in there and, sure enough, there was a huge oil drum of the stuff on a trestle, with a brass ferrule. It was nearly full and when I drained some off into the tin jug hanging under the tap, it ran clear after the first half pint. With so much oil available, it seemed certain that the cottage had not long had electricity and, after rooting around among the tea chests, I found half a dozen good quality oil lamps that must have served the rooms, and a couple of hurricane lamps that could be used as portable lanterns. All these I carried carefully indoors and spent the rest of the day cleaning and polishing them, replacing the old oil and trimming the wicks. By early evening, I had all of the lamps working and, although the smell was initially a bit overpowering, it decreased as they warmed up.

I was so pleased with these lamps that I resolved there and then to use them instead of my electric lights. Not only was their light, once adjusted, soft and gentle but they gave off considerable heat that would be welcome in winter and, of course, I'd save money.

Over the course of the next week, my eyes grew used to the softer, dimmer light and I preferred it to the harsh white electric lights. Coming back from the pub gave me the chance to try out the suggested techniques for improving night vision but as the skies were mainly clear and the moon and stars visible, I could see reasonably well anyway. Even when the moon was new or hidden behind the clouds for a while, there was usually enough starlight to see my way.

I did not venture into the wood again after dark.

Pub visits were becoming more frequent, encouraged partly by the pleasant early spring weather and partly by my ability to drink alcohol after years on medication and, though I did not choose to mix with the 'locals' very much, I did, at least, pass the time of day with them. More than just a polite 'Good evening' seemed to encourage their innate curiosity that, to me, seemed more like nosiness, and the briefest conversations always led to questions about me, which I did not like.

More or less every night, there was a themed event; often

it was live music but there were televised football matches and, of course, darts, dominoes and quiz nights. Only the music appealed to me. One such event was a 'spiritual' evening with a tarot card reader and a lady clairvoyant. I'd seen it advertised at the post office and, although I don't believe a word of any of it, I wanted to consult the clairvoyant just because I had never been to one before and, being new to the area, I could be sure there would be no trickery.

Arriving early, I ordered a pint and stayed at the bar so that I could book my slot with the clairvoyant's assistant – a smart young man who also collected the fee in advance. It seemed that learning about the future was an expensive business.

Before I could hand over this exorbitant amount of cash, strident cries rang out from behind me. At a table near the front of the pub, a heavily built middle-aged woman exotically made up with slabs of mascara around her eyes and a long, dyed hairpiece held high on her head by a sort of Spanish comb, was screeching and pointing at me. Apparently, I found out later, she considered me to be some sort of emissary of evil, the Antichrist, and was threatening to walk out if I didn't leave the pub immediately! The pub was crowded and most people seemed to be looking at me. I felt myself blushing uncontrollably and couldn't think what to do next. The young assistant was giving me my money back and the barmaid had come from behind the counter and was in deep discussion with the clairvoyant who appeared on the edge of hysteria. She returned to the bar and, with some embarrassment, said: 'I'm sorry, er, Jack, isn't it? Madame ZaZa seems to be a bit… er… spooked by you and won't stay if you remain here.' She leaned closer and whispered, 'A bit of a publicity stunt if you ask me but, be a dear – I'll give you a couple of pints on the house if you take it out to the beer garden to drink.'

I agreed, of course, desperately wishing to avoid everyone's attention and hide in the shadows. I took my pints and walked quickly to the back of the pub, followed still by the shrieks of Madame ZaZa and wondering why, if she were a clairvoyant, she hadn't known I would be there.

A bit shaken and rather embarrassed by this strident rejection, I beat a hasty retreat to the beer garden and its wide, open-fronted marquee. Peeved, I finished my beer and decided to leave, loitering only to let my eyes get accustomed to the much dimmer lighting in the tent. A man, who I knew only as Mark, passed my table and asked me why I was not taking my turn with the 'medium'.

'Oh, she won't tell *me* my fortune,' I called after him as he entered the crowded bar. 'But I will!' came a woman's voice from the darkness at the back of the beer garden.

Squinting into the gloom, I could just make out the shape of a woman seated at the last table, against the shrubs at the back of the awning. As I was the only other person in the beer garden, the remark was obviously meant for me and I stood up, hesitantly, but out of sheer curiosity walked over towards the table where I was just able to discover her outline in the darkness there. She motioned me to sit down and by the flickering light of a candle in a jam jar on the rough wooden table, I could just make out a young woman dressed in black, facing me across the dim flame. She didn't speak and I took time to study her more closely. Before me sat a lady in her late twenties, perhaps, with long dark hair framing a rather triangular face that reminded me of old photographs of Victorian aristocrats except that her thick, dark eyebrows slanted upwards at the corners, her full lips in a half smile, revealing large and even white teeth. In all, a most unusual face but certainly strikingly attractive.

The continuing silence became awkward and so I ventured a clumsy introduction. 'I'm Jack. Did you say you would read my fortune?'

'Not *read*,' she corrected, 'but tell you about yourself.'

The smile disappeared and she arched her eyebrows awaiting my reply.

'Well, I'd like that but, if you believe that "medium", it's not without its risks.' Laughing, I nodded towards the open pub door through which Madame ZaZa was just visible. 'She thinks I'm evil,' I added, still laughing.

'She's a fool, a fake, a self-deluded idiot,' she sneered. Such venom surprised me but I made no comment, believing the description apt. 'So, Jack,' she said, 'or would you prefer "Jacques"? And should I speak French to you?' This really took me aback because I had never mentioned my upbringing in Paris to anyone in the village. Not waiting for a reply, she continued: 'So, English it is then. Give me your hand, Jack.' I presented my hand, palm upwards. She slapped it and then grasped it in cold, bony fingers. 'I don't want to read it, just hold it.'

To hide my embarrassment, I tried to sound casual. 'Oh, you work on sensory perception then?'

'No. I just wanted to hold your hand,' she whispered, giving it a gentle squeeze.

Surprised and delighted, I believed I was making unexpected progress with this most unusual and exotic lady. It seemed certain that she was trying to attract me. Not knowing quite how to show my reciprocal interest, I held her hand a little more tightly than necessary.

'You have a troubled mind,' she announced, serious now. 'A recent event has greatly shaken you. You are full of self-doubt.' Suddenly, she looked up at me and her dark eyes seemed to penetrate my very soul. 'I can help you with that…' Her voice trailed away. She fell silent but continued to stare at me in such a direct way that I felt very uncomfortable and looked away. 'Look at me, Jack! Look into my eyes! Why are you so afraid of me? Do I displease you?' Her features were becoming hard to discern in the gathering dark.

I was becoming aware of a slight foreign intonation in her deep voice and slightly odd turn of phrase and remembered that she had offered to speak French. 'Displease me? Heavens, no. Quite the reverse in fact.' It sounded forced but I didn't know what else to say.

'Then look at me!' she commanded again.

I don't know why I found it so difficult to hold her eyes. Somehow, she intimidated me. I wasn't used any more to being the centre of anyone's attention. She pushed her face closer to mine and whispered: 'We will be friends, will we not?'

As she moved, I became aware of a strange, musky fragrance, unusual but not unpleasant, and that seemed to be her natural scent rather than a perfume.

In spite of all of the beer I had drunk and its dulling effect on my mind, I realised that I was already enchanted with this woman in a way that I had never experienced before and my immediate thoughts were to make an effort to show her that I was interested before my abnormal reticence drove her away.

'A drink?' I enquired, lamely, thinking that I could also use the trip to the bar as an opportunity to relieve myself of some of my intake of Guinness. She merely shook her head and left me not knowing what to say next.

'Well, *I* could go another pint – are you sure you won't…?'

'Certain.'

'OK. I'll only be gone a moment…'

When I returned, clutching my beer, a few moments later, she was gone. Deeply disappointed, I ran to the road in front of the pub but there was no one to be seen in the lane in either direction. Depressed and deflated, I retraced my steps and found Mark – a local who always spoke to me – in good spirits propping up the bar. He grinned at me. Apparently, Madame

ZaZa had given him good news and booked him for a personal reading later that week.

'Mark, that woman I was talking to in the garden when you came past, do you know who she is?' It was so stupid that I had not even asked her name.

'Woman, old son? Who was that then?'

'That's what I'm asking *you*,' I said, trying to keep the exasperation from my voice. He looked confused.

'I didn't see any woman, Jack.'

'Come on, I was talking to her when you asked me why I wasn't at the bar, or at least just afterwards.' Mark still looked puzzled.

'Oh, *then*. Well, I thought you were on your own. Didn't see anyone else.'

He grinned foolishly and I guessed he'd had a lot to drink. Irritated, I pushed past him and caught the barmaid's eye.

'Frankie, that lady I've been talking to outside, do you know her name?'

She looked at me oddly.

'I didn't notice any lady with you, Jack. I'm sorry.'

She moved away and I guessed that Mark had put her up to playing this trick on me. The pub had virtually emptied now and I realised with despair that it was past midnight and the street lamps would be off – another long walk home in the dark. Even the novelty of pursuing my experiments with night vision did not make the prospect of the walk any more attractive and I slunk away with bad grace.

Once on the road, the first few minutes were not that bad; the air was cool and bracing and the vicinity of the pub was reasonably well lit. Once around the bend and out of sight, it was a different matter. The cool air seemed to turn colder and my previously confident strides became slower and hesitant. I tried to concentrate on the darkness ahead but with little positive result and began to think that future experimentation should be abandoned and an electric torch purchased. None of that could help my present circumstances. I just had to keep going. Fortunately, the beer I'd consumed during the long evening served to lift my spirits a bit and by reflecting happily on my conversation with the mystery woman, I covered several hundred yards without realising it. Why on earth had I not asked her name?

The going was now slightly downhill and I was drawing near to the crossroads that formed the centre of the village and where the zebra crossing gave an intermittent yellow light from two beacons. Adjacent to this stood the village bus shelter. Buses being very few and far between, the shelter was not particularly elaborate and looked more like an open-fronted shed. It did have a pitched roof though and a bench seat against the back wall. It was, of course, pitch black inside but as I came level with it, a sudden voice startled me.

'I have been waiting for you.'

Although I recognised it as belonging to my recent lady companion, I still gave an involuntary start. Turning towards the sound, I stared into the blackness of the shelter's interior. Unable at first to see anything there, I moved forward cautiously and the light from the crossing beacons fell into the shelter revealing the vague outline of a woman seated back against the rear wall. A step closer and I could make out the pale face appearing and disappearing in the strobe effect of the flickering beacons.

Wanting to greet her politely, I felt hampered by not knowing her name and said, lamely: 'Oh, it's you. You gave me quite a scare. Why did you leave the pub without saying goodbye?' I couldn't keep the hint of a reproach out of my voice.

'Pubs are not my favourite places… too many people…' Her voice trailed off.

I thought of the deserted beer garden with just the two of us.

'Come and sit down beside me.' I did as she asked, advancing carefully in the dark and feeling for the seat before sitting down.

Perhaps her eyes had become more accustomed to the gloom because she seemed to be able to see me much better than I could see her. She took my hand and I felt again how cold she seemed. The pleasant musky scent increased and I guessed she was leaning closer to me. I felt her head on my shoulder and smelled the fragrance of her hair as she cuddled up to me.

Surprised yet delighted by this sudden unexpected turn of events, I reacted slowly, moving closer to her. She moved her arm behind my head and suddenly she was kissing me with a passion that took me completely by surprise. Still slow to react, I put my arms around her and, as best I could, returned her embrace. In spite of the dark, cool night and the several pints of beer I'd had, I began to feel physically aroused. I couldn't remember the last time I had made love to a woman – before the 'Event' certainly, and I hadn't realised how much I now needed that release. I could feel her big white teeth against my lips and that pleasant musky smell, and the pent up feeling of all those months alone surged up in me. One thing was rapidly leading to another when, to my dismay, I heard voices outside. It seemed that the last few drunken revellers from the pub were descending the hill towards our shelter. My lady friend heard them too and leapt up with a speed that surprised me.

'I must go, Jacques…!'

'Wait!'

'I cannot. Don't look for me; I will find you.'

And with that, to my complete dismay, she was gone into the blackness. I felt sure that if we had kept quiet, the drunks would not have seen us and passed by. That, in fact, was what they did, leaving me to resume my journey frustrated, disappointed and annoyed.

By the time I arrived home, however, I was starting to see the positive side of things. I had met a beautiful if somewhat strange and mysterious woman and it seemed very much as though she liked me too. By the time I crawled into bed, I felt that my life was at last taking an upward turn.

It must have been near to three in the morning when my bladder woke me and forced me out of bed. I had forgotten to draw the curtains and, naked, I decided not to light the lamp. Passing a small window on my way back from the bathroom, I happened to glance outside; the sky had cleared and the starlight was bright enough to cast a dim light on the front garden. Just for a moment, I thought I saw a dark figure glide across the lawn towards me. I stood back from the window into the greater darkness of the narrow hallway and watched with unease the outline of a face approaching the leaded glass panes. I must have given an involuntary start or made some slight sound because, in the blink of an eye, the figure disappeared. I moved to another window from where I could see the road and gate but there was no one there.

Shivering, I jumped back into bed, pulling the covers tightly around me. I was cold and more than a little unnerved until I decided that it was just a trick of the half light shining through the moving branches of the tall trees surrounding my garden. Eventually, I fell into a fitful sleep full of disturbing images and was relieved to get up with the sun and make some coffee.

I hummed a tune while the coffee boiled and felt happier and more relaxed than I had done for many months.

Whatever the circumstances of our unexpected and rudely interrupted meeting, it seemed that I had found a beautiful girl (or rather, she had found me) who appeared to be attracted to me. I had never been courted in such an intriguing and exciting way and even the fact that I knew nothing about this new friend, not even her name, could not dampen the exhilaration that I felt. It would have been nice to have planned my next move but as I knew neither who she was nor where she came from nor, indeed, where she went, it seemed impossible. Her last words to me were to *not* look for her. It was the mystery and unexpected train of events that most intrigued me and she must have been aware of this effect and using it as part of her 'technique'. It was certainly different from anything I had previously experienced.

Putting down my coffee, I went out through the front door to collect the two milk bottles I was having delivered every other day and, in turning to come back in, I happened to glance at the lawn: from the tall front hedge was a track – or, rather, two tracks left in the dew on the grass. Though smudged, they looked a lot like footprints and led to the small bay window, returning once more to the hedge. Presuming they must have been made by a large dog or perhaps slurred in the dew by a fox, I remembered what I thought I had seen through the window in the early hours of the morning.

None of this succeeded in diverting my thoughts from 'Ligeia' whom, for want of her real name, I had christened my lady friend of the previous night, for no other reason than she reminded me of the woman in Poe's famous story. Meeting her had already started to fill a void in my new life that I had not really been aware of until then. Sitting in the old, battered leather chair looking out at my garden lit by the early morning sun, I felt a peace and a calmness that I had not experienced since long before the 'Event'.

Of course, the first thing I did on reaching the pub that evening was to check on the beer garden. There was no sign of 'Ligeia' there so I returned to the bar, bought a pint and then chose the secluded table at the back of the garden where we had met the previous night and settled down to wait.

Nothing much happened for a long time. Various 'locals' arrived and left (using the back door was a status symbol reserved for a select few long-standing customers) and I made frequent trips to the bar to replenish my glass.

It felt weird to be so smitten so quickly by such a strange woman and yet not even know her name. She seemed an accomplished actress, whoever she was, and her seduction techniques highly unusual and, as far as I was concerned, very effective. You would think that any woman looking as strikingly unusual as she did and who behaved in such a strange, almost furtive way, would be known to everyone in such a small village. Yet my careful and tactful questions had brought no response – at least, not from anyone in the pub. Nor did it seem as though they were hiding anything or playing a joke on me, but rather that they genuinely did not know whom I was talking about. Tonight, I was bent on getting some answers from her, if she showed up that is, and as it got later and later, that wasn't looking hopeful.

Night had fallen and I was on my final pint, about to go home, when I heard my name being called from the dense shrubs that joined the garden to the lane. My spirits rose immediately but I tried not to show how elated I felt, finished my pint and strode nonchalantly in the direction of the calls. There were no lights on the side wall of the pub but I could just make out the vague outline of a figure on the opposite side of the lane, away from the direct light cast by the front windows. Surprisingly, no one else seemed to have heard her calls. As soon as I came near her, that musky, pervasive fragrance confirmed her identity.

Although it was a warm night, she felt cold. Dressed, as far as I could see, in a thin, dark summer dress, she seemed unaware of how cool her skin felt and her arm around my neck and her face pressing my cheek quite alarmed me until I remembered how cold she had seemed before when she had held my hand and when we kissed.

After a long greeting kiss, she stood back, took my hand and began to speak French to me – soft, educated French with a trace of a Parisian accent.

Guiding me back along the lane in the direction I would take to go home, she chatted excitedly about how much she had looked forward to seeing me and how sorry she was that she had come so late. She did not, however, offer any explanation.

'Hey, hey, *attend!* (wait!)' I replied to her in French as soon as I could get a word in.

'Listen, we need to talk – talk about you…'

'Me?' she feigned surprised.

'Yes, you, *ma biche* (my dear).' I told her how frustrated I was that I didn't even know her name, while she seemed to know a lot about me.

'It's not important, Jacques, but if you must know, it's Manon!'

'So you are French then…?'

She smiled. 'Not exactly. But I like to speak the language! So romantic, don't you think?'

Answering my questions with a question of her own was not getting us very far.

'Look, Manon, I really do want to know you better…'

She interrupted: 'I think, Jacques, that you will soon know me very well… at least in the biblical sense of that word.'

She giggled and snuggled up to me. I didn't want to spoil the mood but I persisted: 'Look, Manon, let's be practical for a minute. I would like to have a relationship with you…'

'A relationship?' she asked, unable to keep the amusement out of her voice. 'What a quaint expression!' She started laughing and I felt a trace of annoyance that she found it so amusing to parry my attempts at serious conversation. I must have sighed my frustration because she immediately seemed to sense my growing impatience.

'OK, OK, *mon grand*, I'll be serious if that is what you want but you are not going to get all clingy and possessive with me, are you?'

I didn't want to risk upsetting her and said: 'I wouldn't dare. I don't want to change… er… how we are, but surely it's reasonable for me to want to know more about you, my lady of the night. I mean, where do you live? No one around here knows you…?'

'Have you been asking about me then, Jacques?'

There was a sudden serious edge to her voice, which warned me to play down my inquisitiveness and I hastened to reassure her: 'No, not at all, but it would be nice to know how to contact you.'

She stopped teasing me then.

'Yes, of course, and I'm sorry for playing games with you, Jacques.'

Her sudden about-face surprised me. Taking my hand again, she pulled me forward.

'Come. I'll show you.'

Off we went again, faster now. I was already convinced my lovely companion could see in the dark but, luckily for me, the moon had come out from behind the clouds and the whole area was clothed in a cold, silvery light. I watched Manon from behind as she led the way. Very tall, very slim, hair reaching down her back to her waist, her angular frame seemed to lope along, reminding me somehow of the paintings of strange beings that adorn the walls of ancient Egyptian tombs, broad-shouldered and narrow-waisted. Suddenly, she plunged to the right. The tall hedge that bordered the lane ended just for a few feet in what appeared to be a gap leading to an overgrown path that could once have been a drive wide enough for a car but was now barely wide enough for two people to walk side by side. I'd never noticed the gap before though I must have passed it many times, going to and from the pub. But then it wasn't lit in any way and easily missed in the dark.

The going was uneven and felt like gravel that grass and weeds had grown up through, and water had eroded holes here and there. From what I could see in the moonlight, the track curved left and then right so we soon lost sight of the lane. Manon had fallen silent but once we were out of view from the road, she slowed down and resumed her hold around my waist.

'Where are…?'

'To my place,' she cut in quickly.

After what seemed like ten or even fifteen minutes' walking in silence, we came to some tall, wrought iron gates that must have been magnificent in their early days but now, even by moonlight, I could see were rusty with the dark green paint flaking off. They were a presage of what was to come. Once through, rising in front of us and filling the whole view from left to right was a huge house – a manor house of some style except that it was falling down. The great façade showed signs of long decay and even by the dim light, I could see that the left wing nearest to us was partly in ruin; everything around it was falling down and even the surrounding moat was choked with undergrowth and full of reeds. The moon came out from behind the clouds and shone down from the jagged roof line, a ghastly pale light upon the creepy, seemingly derelict, building.

Manon did not appear to notice the surprise and uneasiness I felt and pulled me along a weed-grown, brick path that skirted the building, terminating in a tall, ivy-covered brick wall. She pushed at an old oak door set in an arched frame and we found ourselves in what must once have been a beautiful walled garden but was now not far removed from a jungle.

'This was my favourite place,' she told me, 'but since my parents died, it's gone to ruin.' She added bitterly: 'Like everything else.'

'Your parents died? I'm so sorry, Manon.' Now I knew her name, I could not stop using it.

'It's OK. It was quite a time ago.'

'So now you live here all alone?' I asked incredulously. She looked at me for a long time before replying, as if my curiosity disturbed her and she was trying to decide on an answer that would not prompt any further probing on my part.

'No,' she said at last. 'With... Eloïse.' She added the name almost as an afterthought.

Suddenly, as if she felt she had said too much, she turned round and led me back through the arched door and along to the rusty entrance gates. She must have seen the surprise on my face and said quickly, 'I'm sorry, Jacques, I can't ask you to come in... not tonight... I'll walk you back to the lane... it's become very dark again...'

I was choked. I'd waited all evening to see this girl, felt I was really getting somewhere with her and now suddenly I seemed to be getting the 'brush-off'. Reluctant to give up on what promised to be a good night, I kept hold of her hand, cuddled her and whispered: 'Well, why not come home with me, Manon? After all, your place does seem a bit... er...

unwelcoming tonight. There are no lights on and…' She placed a cold, bony finger on my lips.

'Shh, shh! Don't be offended, Jacques. I'm not trying to get rid of you, I promise, it's just that… well, tonight I have to pack some clothes for Paris in the morning.'

'You're leaving?' I asked in dismay.

'Only for a few days. I have some family business to sort out there… papers to sign. Otherwise… I would ask you to come with me…' She started to laugh. 'You're jealous now, aren't you? I bet you love Paris as much as I do. It's a hard place to leave once you've lived there a while. Look, don't be sad, I'm sorry. We will do it together next time.'

Well, that at least was a consolation. Paris with Manon!

We had reached the lane again and she gave me a long, passionate goodnight kiss and promised to find me as soon as she got back.

I went off into the night reasonably placated and anxious to reach my cottage while the moonlight was still fending off the darkness.

Throughout the next day, I thought a lot about Manon and dreamed about her the following night. The whole idea of moving to this isolated cottage was to cut myself off from people and relationships. After the 'Event', I swore I'd never get involved with anyone else. When I fall in love, I know that I can become a bit obsessive about it and I just didn't want to feel that pressure again, at least not yet. I did feel lonely, it is true, so much so that I'd even given thought to perhaps a closer relationship with Lorca… I mean, she was attractive in her way. Of course, I had no idea how she would have felt about it and I was sensible enough not to make any advances. In any case, to be rejected would have set me back in trying to regain my self-esteem and a positive response from her would completely change our relationship and complicate my life while my grip on things was still quite fragile.

Manon, I felt, would be different. We could just be friends. But even while I was considering that, I knew I was deluding myself. In the old days I understood enough about myself to realise that I didn't 'do' friends – not with women anyway and not with men at all. It had always been all or nothing – total love or no relationship at all. I hated being like that but it didn't seem as though I could change. Already I was becoming a bit obsessed with Manon, wondering what she was doing in Paris at any given moment, jealous of who she might be with and imagining I was there with her, laughing and flirting together, falling in love in the 'beautiful city'.

There was no respite from these 'daydreams' and no way to stop them and, for the first time, I considered whether stopping my medication was aggravating the situation. Anyway, I just had to go along with the ride and see where it took me. I was beginning to realise that isolation may not be the answer to my problems despite what the psychiatrist had promised me. Of course, I trusted her implicitly but I felt her diagnosis might be wrong on this occasion.

After churning all this over in my mind, I concluded that, as Manon had taken all the initiative so far in our relationship, it would be a good thing if I became a little more assertive and cast around to think of what I could do to please her.

Suddenly, as I was planting some shrubs, I thought how overgrown her favourite place, the walled garden, had been when she took me to the manor and, without thinking it through, I resolved immediately to do something about it. I could surprise her with a much nicer garden to use when she came back from Paris.

As soon as Lorca had finished and called out '*la revedere* (goodbye),' I picked up my spade and secateurs and headed down the lane, reasoning that larger tools, wheelbarrows, rakes and so forth would be available in the myriad of outbuildings I had noticed at the manor.

Chapter 3

'The scariest monsters are the ones that lurk within our souls.'
Edgar Allan Poe

It was obvious that this part of the old walled garden had not been in use for many years. The rhododendrons and other large shrubs made a tall circular hedge around an old, unrecognisable statue in the centre of a huge, corroded, lead-sided raised pool, and grass had spread across the dark gravel paths that converged on it from the four points of the compass. The whole garden was fringed with dark pines, giving it a permanent green back-drop. The small, central lawn had become a thick matted carpet dotted with moss, dandelions and self-sown forget-me-nots, so that it was hard to know where the edges met the gravel paths choked with docks and small briars. The air was warm and sultry with the sort of leaden sky that usually preceded a storm.

Stripping to the waist, I attacked the paths first, pulling up the tufts of grass and clumps of docks and edging the lawn with a spade. Soon it became even hotter and the air so warm that it was difficult to breathe. Heavy clouds blocked out the sun and gave the garden a gloomy, oppressive, almost sinister aspect and a depressing atmosphere.

Fortunately, along with some sandwiches for lunch, I'd had the foresight to bring some bottles of beer and drank from them the whole time I was working. Finally, too hot to continue, I slumped down on an ancient, cast-iron bench in a sort of alcove formed by rotting wooden trellis. The smell of dampness and decay was everywhere. I fished out the last bottle of beer that I'd put to cool in the brackish green water of the lead pool and that, together with the exertion and the heat, must have encouraged me to fall asleep soon after I sat down.

Waking suddenly, I was momentarily at a loss to know where I was and when I finally realised, I was alarmed to find such a change in everything. The air was still sultry but a warm breeze had sprung up and was driving heavy grey clouds across the sky. The pine trees had turned from dark green to almost black and thunder rumbled ominously in the distance accompanied by a scattering of increasingly heavy drops of rain. By the time I had gathered up my clothes and tools, the scattered raindrops had become a heavy shower and lightning flickered at the edges of the sky. Confused, I sought the path that had led me to the central part of the garden but my work and the ever-thickening raindrops had changed the scenery so much that it disorientated me. By the time I had located the right path, it was hard to see more than a few feet through the heavy curtain of hissing raindrops and the rapidly gathering gloom. More by luck than judgement, I staggered out through the oak door in the wall and kept going until I felt I was nearing the old house and had the luck to stumble on to the loose gravel of the driveway.

I had originally intended to follow the drive out on to the lane and then head for home but it soon dawned on me that the pub was much nearer and a more agreeable place to shelter. Sadly, it was not to be. The sky opened and a solid sheet of water descended in front of me, accompanied by a loud clap of thunder that, although I was expecting it to follow the lightning flash, still made me jump. My only chance of shelter now was the dilapidated porch of the house itself. Turning round, abandoning my tools, I sprinted towards the ruinous manor. The downpour was by then so intense that the raindrops stung my body in spite of my shirt, and my jacket was already soaked over my arm before I could get it on. It was almost dark now because of the heavy clouds and gathering dusk and I could have done with a light to guide me. Manon was away in France and not likely to leave lights on. The house would be locked but the roofed porch was an open affair, a bit like the entry to a church, with a bench seat either side. A bolt of lightning briefly lit the arched entrance as I staggered in and flung myself down on one of the side benches. The next roll of thunder suggested the storm was nearly overhead.

I lay still, the water draining off me onto the rough stone floor, listening to the loud swish of the rain and the dull splash of the torrents of water coming off the roof and out of the overflowing gutters.

After being so hot all day, I was now feeling cold; soaked through, I began to shiver and looked in vain for any let-up in the storm. As my eyes adjusted to the gloom of the porch, I noticed with astonishment that the huge old oak front door stood slightly ajar, yet I could have sworn that it was tightly closed when I first came in from the rain. I squinted and looked again. It was definitely open about six inches.

An immense clap of thunder made me jump and for a moment I looked back at the sheet of rain in the garden. There was no way I could walk home in that, or even to the pub – it wasn't just the intense rain, I was wet through already – it was simply that it was impossible to see more than a few feet in front of me. Except for the flashes of lightning, it was pitch black and not even the edges of the drive were discernible.

And then there was that open door. I was certain that Manon had said she would be in Paris for a couple of days so how could the door be ajar? They would never have left it that way and I did not remember it being like that when I arrived. A break-in? Burglars perhaps? I couldn't, in all decency, leave the place unlocked and vulnerable like that. On the other hand, if I went in, I could justify my presence as concern about security and take shelter at the same time.

I pushed the heavy old door and it swung back soundlessly into the black tunnel of the hallway. The darkness there was absolute and, never having been in the house and with no idea of the layout, I hesitated to advance. Moments later, a flash of lightning lit the porch way and a split second of light fell on the hall floor enough to reveal the presence of a wide staircase on the right and a long corridor to the left of it. The following peal of thunder seemed to shake the very fabric of the house and roll with an almighty crash off the roof just above my head. I stood stock still, not daring to move for fear of colliding with something and waited for more lightning to guide me to a light switch. The rain hissed angrily, slanting into the open porch that I'd just left, but not one glimmer of light penetrated the hall.

Cold and wretched in my saturated clothes, I couldn't wait any longer and began carefully to grope my way along the wall, guessing that a switch would be positioned near the door. The walls felt cold and clammy and a strong odour of dampness hung on the air, as from an empty house shut up and long since unoccupied. Thinking the switch must be on the opposite wall between the staircase and the front door, I reluctantly swung my hands away from the damp plaster and very carefully and infinitely slowly, hands held out in front, inched towards the stairs – or rather the place I had glimpsed them to be in the lightning flash.

Once away from the wall, I was lost. The blackness was complete and though I held my hands out at arm's length and turned around very slowly, nothing seemed in reach. Now I was not sure which way I was facing and, as in the wood a few weeks ago, I felt a rising panic at being so completely surrounded by darkness.

If I could have been sure which way led to the door, I would have run out, even into the pouring rain, such was my apprehension. Carefully, I moved forward in the direction I guessed the front door might be and suddenly touched something cold and clammy. Snatching my hand away, I fought the instinct to run, knowing that I would be sure to collide with a wall or even the half-closed door itself. Forcing down my panic and thinking rationally, I tried squinting into the blackness and then opening my eyes as wide as possible to achieve the maximum light at my retinas. Whether I just imagined I saw it, I can't say, but my mind reasoned that at that height, I had touched the wooden banisters of the stairs.

Infinitely slowly and cautiously, I stretched out my hand again and felt the object with the tips of my fingers. It was smooth and shaped and had edges and so I concluded that I had been right – this was the banister. Though relieved, I was still desperate to find a light switch. With my left hand grasping the rail, I moved my foot forward until it made contact with the bottom riser of the uncarpeted stairs, stretched my right hand out to where the right-hand wall should be and was rewarded with the feel of smooth, cold plaster. Logically, the front door should now be directly behind me and if I stepped backwards carefully, moving my hand along the wall at about shoulder height, I should eventually find a light switch situated at the beginning of the stairs.

It seemed to take an age and the darkness was almost palpable, like a black fog resting on my shoulders. Once I'd touched the architrave of the door frame, I moved my hand down the wall and then back up until, by some miracle, I found the cold dome of a brass and porcelain switch. My fingers found the toggle and flicked it down. And behold, there was light! Dazzling at first, it soon dimmed to the weak light of a 40-watt bulb with no shade, hanging on its plaited flex about midway down the hallway. But to me it was salvation.

I was now able to make out my surroundings – at least in the immediate vicinity, though anything more than twenty feet away was still in shadow and only the lower half of the stairs could be seen. The slashing sound of the rain at the door behind me took my immediate attention and I saw, with dismay, that sheets of rain were slanting deeper into the open porch and even splashing onto the hall floor. Pushing the door closed, I realised that I had to make a decision: go back out into the rain and darkness and hope to find the driveway and then the lane or wait where I was, in the hope that conditions would improve as the storm passed. If I ventured further into the house, I might find dry clothes and, if very lucky, a raincoat and torch. While considering these options, I remembered that I was actually supposed to be checking on the security of Manon's house and, whatever happened, I could not leave it unlocked.

Reluctantly, and very grateful to have light, I penetrated deeper into the hallway. Most of the right side was taken up by the wide stairway but there was a dark painted door on the left that I guessed led into a front room with the huge overgrown bay window that I had seen when I arrived that morning.

Passing this, I saw another that would lead, I thought, to a back room giving out onto the rear garden. Under the recess made by the stairs, I saw a door on the right but in front of me, at the very end of the hallway, was a wide door that, logically, would lead to a back kitchen. In fact, it was a dining room but a double door on the right of this room seemed likely to be the entrance to the kitchen. Unfortunately, the dim light from the dining room's single bulb did not extend far into the kitchen and I had to grope around a bit for a light switch in there.

Sparsely furnished and austere, it contained only the bare necessities: a grubby gas stove with plate rack above, a metal cupboard with wire mesh that must have been a meat safe and a long, scrubbed but dusty, pine table with a couple of matching benches. None of it seemed to be in use. The focal point along the only window was a huge butler sink with heavy slate drainers and a single tap surrounded by rusty stains, left probably by an earlier iron hand pump. Surprised at the lack of any modern amenities, I reasoned that I was probably in an old wing of the house, largely disused, and that somewhere in the depths of this huge old building was a modernised wing with an elaborate modern kitchen and comfortable rooms used by Manon.

I left a trail of water dripping from my hair and saturated clothes and though the atmosphere of the storm was initially close and sultry, the house seemed cold and chilly and I started to shiver. Casting about for a towel, I found some old wiping up cloths in a drawer and, to my delight, a long, man's coat on a hook on what must have been the back or garden door. The coat, like the room, smelled musty, damp and rather unpleasant but was a whole lot better than my saturated shirt and jacket.

Back in the hall, I tried the door behind the stairs. I couldn't find a light switch but the glimmer from the dim bulb in the hall revealed tall bookcases full of old leather-bound books, the spines of which were dusted with a green-grey mould.

Next, I tried the remaining door to the left of the kitchen. The light switch was to hand but did not work and again it was the poor light from the hall that allowed me to make out old, leather armchairs and a deep, dark coloured carpet. The musty smell pervaded all these rooms and convinced me that they were long since unlived in and that this part of the house was probably not kept locked as it was deserted and had little of value to steal.

Outside, the rain was still falling in sheets and the thunder and lightning so frequent that it seemed the centre of the storm was overhead. The rain reminded me that I needed to use the toilet and it seemed obvious that the bathroom must be upstairs. Reluctantly, I started up the dusty bare wooden treads, which felt damp and slippery, and the stale air and musty smell increased with each step. And so did the darkness. The last few steps were in total blackness and as soon as I reached the landing I started to grope the walls for a light switch. Finally, my fingers touched the cold brass and porcelain of a switch and I flicked it down. To my immense relief a light came on – though the single dim bulb did little to illuminate my surroundings.

Instinctively, I pushed open the door directly across from the stair head and a faint glimmer from white tiles confirmed that it was indeed the bathroom. Again, the light in this room did not work and I struggled to find the toilet in the poor light from the landing. I achieved my purpose more by ear than by sight but the relief was the same.

Instead of returning downstairs, something, curiosity probably, drove me to move back along the landing towards the front of the house. It was long and straight and, within the limits of the sole light bulb, I could just make out the dark recesses of doors leading, I surmised, to bedrooms.

I chose the first door on the left nearest to the landing light above the stairwell and was hit by a cold mustiness as the door creaked open. To my surprise, the switch worked and the naked dim light bulb flickered into life. It was a huge room, sparsely furnished with a large, old-fashioned double bed, a small rough wooden bedside table and a narrow strip of matting on the dusty floorboards alongside the bed.

Moving further in, I could make out the dark shape of a

wardrobe and a wash stand with a basin and ewer. There were no concessions to comfort, no pictures, not even a bedside lamp or bedspread over the thin grey blankets.

Moving out again to the landing, I checked the other bedrooms, at least those whose doors were within the limits of the light. Each was the same except the last and that showed signs of use but only by the fact that the bed appeared to have been slept in, a finding that made me uneasy because I had already convinced myself that I was in an uninhabited part of the house.

As I turned back towards the stairs, suddenly seized with a desire to get out of the place, I could hear that the weather was worsening; the thunder and lightning had diminished but the swish of the rain became a loud drumming on the roof and against the walls of the house – a cloudburst that showed no sign of letting up.

I must have been about halfway back along the passage when the light went out. Once again, I was in intense blackness and I had no way of knowing if it might be a general power cut or only within the system of that house. I forced myself to wait but I knew that the power would not come back on and any thought of finding fuse boxes was out of the question. Even as my eyes became more accustomed to the total darkness, I could see nothing of my immediate surroundings.

Moving cautiously to my right, I stretched out my hand until it came into contact with the damp wall and, advancing very slowly, eventually touched the wooden architrave of a door frame, probably that of the first bedroom I had found.

Entering, I groped for and found the light switch with the faint hope that it was just a blown bulb and that the light in that bedroom would still work. Nothing happened and I knew that I was trapped in the darkness. To attempt to find the stairs and go back down in total darkness would have been very dangerous so I just stood, in impenetrable blackness, just inside the room.

I remembered that the room had been sparsely furnished and the bed had been made, or at least had covers on it. It seemed that my only logical option was to find the bed, take off my saturated and now cold clothes, get under the covers and try to sleep or at least wait out the hours until first light.

Moving cautiously further into the room, I turned, as far as I could judge, slightly to the left towards the centre where I remembered seeing the old double bed. Distances are difficult to judge in the dark and I started to panic, thinking I had overshot the bed and was totally lost in the big room. A lightning flash at the single window was just enough to help me and, in that split second of illumination, I found that I was within inches of the bed and carefully sat down on it.

Peeling off the old coat and my soaked trousers brought welcome relief but I was very cold in spite of the earlier sultry atmosphere. The storm had created a freshness that dropped the temperature by several degrees and I hastened to open the bed clothes.

To my delight, the bed seemed fully made with sheets and at least one blanket and creeping beneath those bedclothes brought a welcome moment of comfort to an unpleasant situation. The sheets felt cold at first but I soon created a little cocoon of warmth and, with that, came a feeling of fatigue, not unpleasant and not unexpected, in spite of the noise of the storm.

The initial damp feel of the sheets evaporated with the warmth of my body and even the musty odour of the room seemed less noticeable. There were only two things on my mind as I drifted off: I should have shut the bedroom door – I can't imagine why I thought that important – and I should have left the light switch down in case the power came back on during the night, although that was pointless too as, now dry and comfortable, I had no intention of moving until dawn.

In spite of the racket outside (the wind that had dropped completely before the rain now seemed to have risen again and was howling around the house), sleep came quickly to me but it was troubled with weird and macabre dreams in which, unsurprisingly, I found myself lost in a dark countryside and seemed to be floating over a strange and desolate land where time meant nothing and where all the things dear to me in this world seemed of no value.

In another dream, I was being chased around the walled garden by sinister, tall, loping figures like Egyptian animal-headed gods. So intense were these nightmares and so real my need to escape them that I woke myself up. It was still pitch dark and I had no means of knowing how long I had been asleep and remained in a sort of half state between waking and slumber.

Then I heard it.

Somewhere in that huge empty house of musty bare rooms and damp, dark passages, something stirred. It was perhaps the gentle closing of a door, near enough to have travelled to my consciousness. I lifted my head from the pillow and concentrated on listening. Above the now distant storm and the hiss of the rain came a quite different sound that, eventually, I identified as footfalls – soft, even stealthy, but definitely footsteps on the bare boards of the landing floor.

As I listened, tense with concentration, the noise gradually increased. Still soft and muffled, the footfalls were definitely coming closer, as if someone or something was moving along the passage towards the bedroom doors.

My first instinct was to jump out of bed: at six feet tall and very fit, I felt I was a match for any burglar, especially as it sounded like a single person. But then reason cut in. Where could I go and what could I do in the total blackness except betray my presence.

And there was something else preventing me – something to do with those footfalls that my brain was telling me was not quite natural. It was stupid, I know, but I couldn't define the uneasiness they caused in me. So, forcing myself to keep absolutely still, I concentrated on the sounds.

The light but relentless increase in the noise indicated that the footfalls were drawing closer to my room. I thought suddenly of the wide-open door and then reasoned that it could not be visible in the total darkness. That reasoning brought other concerns – how could the advancing steps be so sure and steady and confident when nothing could be discerned in the long passageway and there was no sign of a light as from a torch?

I tensed as I judged the steps to be level with my door and waited, heart thumping in my chest, for them to continue along the hall.

To my horror, the footfalls stopped. I held my breath but, though I stared towards where I guessed the open door to be, I could see absolutely nothing in the thick darkness. Then came a sound that made me shiver – a sniff and then several sniffs, like some nocturnal animal scenting out its prey.

Instinctively, I must have held my breath again because I felt myself becoming dizzy. Then, when I felt I could bear it no longer, to my total relief, the footfalls seemed to move on down the hall, or so I thought. My relief was momentary because I soon understood that the footsteps were actually inside the room! Nor could I hope the darkness concealed me for they made unerringly for my bed.

Scared out of my wits, I could think only of flight even though there was nowhere to run to in that dark room or even in the house for that matter, and I was naked and shoeless.

Frozen with fear, I must have hesitated a few seconds, enough to hear an urgently whispered: 'Jacques?' I did not move or speak. It came again. '*Jacques, c'est toi?* (Jack, is that you?)'

So overpowering was my relief that it took me several seconds to croak: 'Manon?'

The next thing I knew was that familiar musky perfume and the bedclothes lifted as she got into bed beside me. Her naked body was cold yet soft and yielding.

'*Je te croyais en France* (I thought you were in France),' I managed to say eventually.

There was silence as I waited for an explanation.

'It's complicated,' she whispered, still speaking in French. As the relief spread through me, I lost all interest in explanations. She was there! She was in bed with me! What did it matter how it came about? She was all over me, urgent and determined, as when she had surprised me in the bus shelter weeks before.

Sitting astride me, she pushed down on my shoulders with her long, cool fingers, her flowing hair brushing my chest as she leaned over me. Her kiss was fierce and passionate and I could feel her big white teeth. My heart was beating fast again but this time not from fear. Weirdly, I felt that she was immensely strong and yet was somehow forcing herself to be gentle with me – a sort of holding-off, as a very strong man does when he holds a child or a delicate woman.

I was calming down now from the shock and fear I had earlier experienced and, as well as arousal, I felt strangely detached, as if floating. She was whispering in my ear in her husky voice, speaking softly in French and moving her cool body against mine with gentle but increasingly provocative movements until I could no longer hold back and rolled her off me onto her back and began to take the initiative myself.

She reached up and put her long fingers on my forehead and immediately I began to experience strange and voluptuous visions: at one point we seemed to be near a deep lily pond in a strange, overgrown garden; at another, we were in soft grass beneath a beautiful tree covered in pink blossom; and then we were somehow flashing through time, first to the past and then to the future, in some insane airborne ride. Nothing of our actual surroundings remained tangible – the dark room, the damp bed, the rough sheets, musty air and rainy night were all banished and replaced by a timeless suspension of belief in things 'real'.

The pleasure seemed to last forever until, suddenly, with the light of dawn, reality came flooding back. My eyes flickered open and by the bright light of a sunny morning knifing through the curtainless window, I saw the shabby, drab, dusty bedroom with its bare wooden floor and sparse old-fashioned furniture. Dust floated in the shafts of sunlight and the musty smell seemed stronger than ever.

As everything came flooding back to me, I turned towards Manon only to find a cold empty space where she had been a short time before. Had it all been a dream? I thought not: her musky perfume pervaded the bed. Determined to find her, I dressed hastily, pulling on clothes that were still damp.

It was surprising how different the house looked in the morning sunlight, with the almost palpable hostility of the night before banished.

After a quick wash in rust-coloured cold water in the bathroom, I skipped downstairs expecting to find Manon in the old kitchen, hopefully making coffee. There was no sign of her there, however, and I concluded that she must be in a modernised wing of the house where she obviously lived.

Finding no connecting door to any other parts of the house, I went outside and walked around the huge old building. Finally, I came to a set of French doors, overlooking the gardens – or, at least, would have done had they not been so overgrown by unkempt shrubs. Everything was locked up tightly and I was unable to see through the dusty glass into what I thought might be a sitting room.

Evidently, the house was empty, leading me to conclude that Manon must have left, probably to buy milk and food. There were no notes fixed anywhere and so, after hanging about for a while in the hope that she would come back, I reluctantly walked up the overgrown drive in the hope that I would meet her on the way.

Everything was still saturated from the night of heavy rain and the puddles were deep and, in some places, right across the drive. Reaching the end of the lane and with no sign of Manon, I turned towards home with a last hope of seeing her at the village shop as I passed. Everything was closed at this early hour and I realised, with a certain resentment, that I would not be seeing Manon. Appearing from nowhere when least expected and disappearing the same way seemed part of her mystique, at least that is what I told myself! The truth was that what had first been intriguing was fast turning into an annoyance – as with everything if you overdo it.

Although the storm had blown itself out, it was far from being a calm day. A blustery breeze blew dark clouds scudding across the sky and the sun struggled to shine occasionally through the gaps. Like the driveway from the house, the lane was heavily puddled and a constant stream of water flowed down each side, unable to enter the overflowing ditches and bringing the leaves blown off the trees, like tiny manic boats. I paid little attention to any of this as my mind was churning like the clouds, with questions occupying most of my attention: how was Manon at home when she told me she would be in Paris? What was she doing in the pitch dark of the derelict wing of the manor house, obviously usually uninhabited? How did this rather shy and bashful girl turn into a sexual predator with seemingly great experience in the art of love-making, as she had been once before when she ambushed me in the bus shelter?

It suddenly occurred to me that darkness might have been the key. Yes, that was it… she *was* shy and bashful but somehow in the cloak of darkness she was able to conquer her reticence and felt able to release her feelings. Or perhaps I had been too long around psychiatrists for my own good.

All these ideas crowded into my mind and, without particularly meaning to do so, I found myself retracing my steps back down the lane to return to the manor, find Manon and persuade her to confide in me and let me help her. I'd nearly reached the waterlogged roadway to the house when I was startled to hear her voice. She appeared next to me wearing the biggest pair of sunglasses I had ever seen.

'Jack! How nice to see you. It's really early… God, you look… er… unwell. What's happened? Did you get caught in the storm?' She was speaking English again. Before I could reply to this barrage of questions, she continued: 'Come back to the house with me. We'll have some coffee. I brought some croissants with me. I hope they'll still be fresh. What a journey! It was fine when I left Paris but by the time I got to Calais for the ferry, it was blowing a force six gale. The crossing was horrible and took twice the usual time so it's taken me a whole night's travelling.'

I didn't know how to answer her. Was she in denial about spending the night with me? Totally confused, I resorted to a tried and tested method I had used in the past – one that had helped me through the trauma of the 'Event': I shut my mouth and let all my mind's questions lie in a heap in another part of my head and then carried on as if nothing had happened. There would be plenty of time to think it all through later; the important thing was what was happening at that moment – she was with me and that was what I wanted.

Her rush of questions over, she seemed to lose interest in any reply from me and we walked in silence back down the path towards the manor. When we reached the gate, she turned to me with a beautiful smile and said simply: 'Jack, a change of plan.' She looked up at the sky as the sun finally broke through the clouds and shone full upon us. She seemed uncomfortable and moved a step into the shade of a tall shrub. 'Look, I'd love to invite you in but after that awful sleepless night on the ferry, I feel utterly wretched. I just want to shower and then go to bed.' She must have seen the disappointment on my face because she added quickly: 'Jack, can we meet at the pub, tomorrow perhaps? I promise I'll be better company.'

What could I say? I was secretly pleased because I wasn't feeling brilliant myself and anyway I needed time to work out how to deal with this crazy split personality thing she seemed intent on pursuing. She leaned forward and planted a quick kiss on my cheeks, French style, and waited pointedly for me to turn back up the path towards the lane.

Although the lane was still flooded here and there, the streams of water running along the edges had slowed considerably and the tinkling sound of the water disappearing through the occasional drain grids was barely perceptible. The sky was clearing, and the sun shining through onto the road caused parts of it to steam and reflect its light in a dazzling way.

I felt buoyed by the return of summer and resolved not to tackle the 'Manon Mystery' until I got home, had a bath and something to eat. But I could not help it. The last part of my walk home went quickly as I pondered the events of the night. It seemed that I must be correct in my assumption that the part of the house where I had taken shelter was not currently lived in but the bed had been made up. Then there was that business about Paris: Manon had definitely told me that she would be away for several days and yet she was there during the night in my bed. Then she appeared later that morning saying that she had had a terrible ferry crossing from Calais. It seemed an elaborate charade just to play a trick on me and, anyway, how could she have known that I would go to the manor or that a storm would force me to stay the night? The more I thought about it, the weirder and more mystifying it seemed. And then there was the love-making. That it was the scariest, most exhilarating and unusual sex that I have ever had was beyond dispute. At the same time, it had been, in some ways, quite frightening in its surprise and its frantic intensity and total silence, alternating between fear and intense pleasure.

I concluded with rising unease that I didn't understand any of it and, though I knew I was falling deeply in love with Manon, she seemed to live two different personalities and it was for me an unsettling experience, no doubt aggravated by my own traumatic experiences prior to the 'Event'. What I didn't need was any sort of relationship with psychiatric undertones, however fascinating being a part of it might be.

With all this buzzing in my head, I walked straight past my cottage and, feeling foolish, I had to retrace my steps.

As I followed the overgrown path to my front door, I thought I saw a quick movement at the front window, as if someone had been looking out and had suddenly stepped back. With my mind so preoccupied, I could not be sure and guessed it might have been Lorca if it was her day to clean. She was the only other person to have a key.

The front door was locked and when I stepped down onto the floor, I called her name. There was no response and it was obvious the place was empty; I mean it was so small that there was nowhere to hide. Nothing seemed out of place or damaged by the storm and I was relieved to see no evidence of the thatch leaking rain through the ceilings. There were just a few damp marks on the kitchen floor tiles that looked a bit like footprints but that I soon dismissed as having been left by the cat who could come and go through a flap in the back door.

In spite of the overnight power cut, there was plenty of hot water and, several cups of coffee and a hot bath later, the chill was at last gone out of my bones. By lunchtime, the sun had steam dried most of the garden and temperatures had risen once again to that of a pleasant late spring day.

I should have been tired after my labour the day before and the various adventures of the night but instead I felt restless and uneasy and could not settle on any of the jobs I attempted in the garden. Somehow I felt that I was missing something – that somewhere exciting events were taking place while I stood in the wings as an observer; quite the opposite of the cosy, closeted security I had, until then, valued in my new home. For the first time in months, I thought about Paris and visualised myself sitting outside at a café table under a tree on a sunlit boulevard drinking wine with a smiling Manon flirting with me as only French girls know how…

'*Mr Jack!*'

The voice startled me and I spun round to face the cottage. Lorca was peering over the closed bottom half of the kitchen door. I'd been unsure if it was her day to clean, or do my washing. That thought set off a chain reaction in my mind. How useless I had become! Before the 'Event', I used to do my own washing, and cooking too, clearing up and making the bed.

By the time I reached Lorca I was feeling quite ashamed of myself.

'*Bona Ziwa, Jack. Ce mai faceţi?*' She was teaching me Romanian but we rarely got beyond the 'Good day, how are you?' greetings.

Her dark eyes bore into mine. She had, it seemed, appointed herself my unofficial guardian, giving her an excuse of sorts for her innate nosiness or 'curiosity' as she called it. Not that she needed an excuse because she was immune to any feelings of tact or subtlety. She examined me, scrutinising everything from the stubble on my face to the dirty jeans I wore to garden. It was silly but I felt myself colour under the intensity of her stare.

'You look terrible, Mr Jack. Like you didn't sleep so much last night,' she said in her quaint English. 'Your bed was not slept in.'

It was a statement but it hinted at a question and she was obviously waiting for an explanation.

'Got caught in the storm,' I offered, determined not to be bullied into providing any details. She was like a priest in a confessional and I could sense her disapproval.

'Pub?' she asked.

Instead of replying to that, I suggested she make a cup of coffee for us both and changed the subject by asking if she had noticed the cat's paw prints on the kitchen floor. I think the word 'paw' escaped her limited vocabulary because she looked puzzled. She latched on to 'cat' though.

'Cat dead,' she said, flatly. She noticed my surprise and added: 'Car kill her, last week.'

I was quite fond of that cat; it wasn't much company and nearly feral but it was a presence in the garden and would occasionally stray into the house, especially when the weather was bad.

'A car? Are you sure, Lorca?'

'Don't know, Mr Jack,' she replied in a bored tone. 'I find her dead on lawn – all, how you say, "cut up"!'

'Cut up?' I repeated mechanically.

'No. Not cut up.' She searched her vocabulary. 'Slashed?' she asked, pleased with the word.

I thought it best to drop the subject and anyway I didn't

want to ask her how she had disposed of the cat in case she told me.

'Mr Jack,' she started again. I knew a reprimand was coming by her tone and because she only called me 'Mr' when she felt some sort of admonition was needed.

'Mr Jack, it not my business but when you have woman here, why you not ask her to do your washing? I have so much to do…'

'Woman, Lorca? What makes you think…?'

'I not *think*, Mr Jack, I know. I smell her scent; I see her footmarks sometimes. Not yours… too small…'

'Lorca, I really have no idea what you're talking about. The only woman who comes in here is *you*!'

She narrowed her eyes at me. It was an obvious gesture of disbelief and somehow it made her look very attractive. Perhaps… if I had not met Manon…

After this odd conversation, Lorca went back to whatever she had been doing in the kitchen, pausing only to pour me a cup of coffee. She sulked a bit after that and sighed loudly from time to time, letting me know that she believed I was lying to her. I left her to it; after all, she'd got it all wrong and my relationship with Manon was none of her business.

The afternoon could not pass quickly enough for me. After Lorca left, I busied myself with clearing up in the garden after the storm and by five o'clock I was eating the salad and cold meat Lorca had left me. Another shower and a shave and I was away to the pub by 8 p.m.

I was not expecting to meet Manon until the next day but I was feeling so pleased with my 'love life' that I needed to celebrate with whomever happened to be in the bar and if by some chance I should bump into Manon…

The storm had now completely blown itself out and given way to a beautiful evening of clear skies and sunshine and the fragrance of freshly washed fields and hedges made my steady walk down towards the pub a very pleasant experience.

Such a contrast to the fears of the night.

BELLE'S DIARY

Friday, 16 July 1971

I forgot to write this up yesterday. Had a headache all day. Probably because of the impending storm. Because of the migraine, I didn't take my medication; it slows me up terribly and makes me feel sort of 'out of it', detached and slow thinking. Good thing is though, I can have a drink tonight. I've had three white wines with ice and if I carry on at this pace, I won't see straight enough to continue this page…

Thursday, 17 July 1971

Feel bad today. Didn't get up until gone 11 a.m. Don't think I did anything stupid at the pub. In fact, it was a fascinating evening. I couldn't have hoped for better proof that my 'powers' are still there in spite of all the medication and that bloody counselling.

It all started quite early in the evening. I'd just gone out into the beer garden and was lighting a roll-up – one of my 'specials' with liquorice paper and a good pinch of Mary Jane – when I spotted that guy, Jack, who's just moved into the thatched cottage. I'd seen him before but this time the old intuition came up good and strong.

It never ceases to amaze me how I see those things –

I've never really understood it either, even though it's been happening since I was a kid. The images jumped up in front of me as soon as he walked past to go into the bar – a sort of tingling in my back and then a very faint aura round his head.

He's very polite. Said 'Good evening' like he meant it. And not so bad looking either. Quite handsome, with a tall, athletic sort of build, wavy brown hair, grey 'come to bed' eyes, and a sort of 'designer' stubble.

But there's something about his eyes that worries me. His past walks with him still, like a shadow but closer.

He got his pint, came back out to the beer garden and smiled when he saw me. But his mind was obviously elsewhere and he scanned the beer garden, seeming to concentrate on the dark areas by the shrubs. After a time, he seemed satisfied that there was no one there and was turning to go back inside until he saw me beckon him over.

He was so polite and shook my hand when I introduced myself. I told him my name was 'Belle': I've always preferred it to Isabelle – it has a sort of informality about it.

Once he was sitting in front of me, I started getting the vibes at max strength. There's no mistake, there's definitely something amiss with him.

What he shows to people is a façade – an elaborate one – but it doesn't fool me. People around here think I'm 'pixilated' but what do they know? They don't have the *gift*.

This guy Jack was good company. I liked him and we clicked and we were soon laughing as though we were old friends. Of course, my being psychic might be unusual but it's not *that* rare and I wondered what he thought of me, whether he was psychic too and could see behind my eyes as I saw behind his.

By the time Mark walked over, we were going great guns. He and Mark are probably the only locals who don't seem to feel any stigma at being seen with me. I noticed though that Jack kept an eye on the rear of the beer garden and it was obvious that he was half expecting someone. His surreptitious vigil lasted the whole evening and even when he got up to go, he couldn't resist a last glance at the bushes around the back of the garden.

Being a bit pissed, I pushed my luck and kissed him goodnight. It was only a peck on the cheek and he took it quite well. I mean, he's more French than he likes to admit and they are all a bit 'touchy-feely', the continentals. He smiled at me showing his nice teeth, made his excuses and left. I have to say that I didn't envy him his walk home. I mean, it's pitch black here at night since the bloody council decided to switch off the street lamps. Not that we had many of them anyway but at least it was something.

So it was a good evening. I'll keep a lookout for him in future. You never know, he might need my services someday. Maybe quite soon.

CHAPTER 4

'By the pricking of my thumbs,
Something wicked this way comes.'
WILLIAM SHAKESPEARE, *MACBETH*

It was so dark when I left the pub after saying goodnight to Belle. Even after waiting a few minutes for my eyes to become accustomed to the night, my vision scarcely improved. The receding glimmer of the pub lights helped a little bit.

My mind was initially busy analysing this new acquaintance, 'Belle'. The name seemed a bit affected but, there again, people do have odd names, especially when, as I suspected, she had chosen it herself. She was probably Isabelle or Maybelle or Annabelle. Names can make a big difference to how you perceive yourself. 'Jack' was OK but I liked the way Manon called me 'Jacques'; it just sounded more romantic somehow. Whatever her given name, Belle seemed nice enough at first though later I thought she was scrutinising me – sort of probing my mind with her eyes and with her questions. It gave me an odd feeling of déjà vu, probably my paranoia unsettled me though. I thought I was done with all that, especially now that I was managing without all the medication. Perhaps I was really a bit peeved that Manon had not made an appearance.

I stopped walking for a moment; I do that sometimes to concentrate my thoughts. My mother used to say that men can't multitask. It seemed obvious that I was getting a bit obsessive about her: Manon, that is. I mean, I could think of little else since the previous night – making love in a creepy old house, in total darkness, during the peak of a storm and with thunder and lightning banging and crashing like the special effects of some old black and white melodrama, with a stunning girl who was trying to violate me! Not exactly a run-of-the-mill experience! When I first moved here, I swore that I'd never get hooked into any more complicated relationships. I meant to give my emotions a complete rest. But I was lonely. It's not natural for me to be solitary. I found that out in prison. I suppose I was still searching for a soulmate. In spite of my good intentions, I was just not cut out to be a loner.

All this deep thinking, on top of several pints of Guinness, had diverted my attention from the task in hand: getting home along this dark lane.

As my concentration returned, I was surprised to find how far I had already travelled. As far as I could estimate, I must be approaching the famous bus shelter. Surely there must be a slight chance that my increasingly nocturnal friend, Manon, would be waiting for me there?

I could soon make out the deeper black shape of the wooden shelter coming up on my right. Something prevented me from entering its thick, heavy darkness. I hesitated in front of it before softly calling her name. The sound seemed swallowed up by the darkness within and so I called a little louder. Again, the sound of my voice seemed not to penetrate; indeed it was almost as if it bounced back, that the darkness was a solid wall.

My whole being was telling me to go, to leave as quickly as possible, and I fought that intuition because it was totally illogical. As I hesitated, I became aware of a fetid, animal smell, somehow warm, emanating from deep inside the shelter. If my mind wanted to stay and debate logic, my body did not, and the adrenalin rush made me take off at a run down the dark tunnel of the lane, scarcely heeding the fact that I couldn't see my hand in front of my face.

Lights in the distance from a slowly approaching car lit up my surroundings for a moment and, turning, I saw my own long shadow stretched along the road behind me. The shadow was clear with sharp edges. And so was the one behind it!

Not sure what I was actually seeing, I looked again, screwing my eyes closed and then opening them very wide. Two shadows! I moved forward and stopped abruptly. The second shadow stopped too but a split second later.

Totally unnerved now, I took off towards the oncoming car, looking over my shoulder every couple of seconds. A bright sweep of light and the car passed me and receded fast, letting the darkness surge back like an incoming tide. My heart was beating so hard in my chest that I felt light-headed.

Forcing myself to think, I considered whether someone from the pub was following me. I called out, my voice shaking, but received no reply. Deep in the recesses of my brain, my primitive instinct was telling me to run – and that's what I did.

So thick and impenetrable was the darkness that the only thing that kept me on the road was the feel of the tarmac under my feet. Whenever I stopped for a few seconds to catch my breath and to listen, the footsteps behind me stopped too but fractionally later than mine. I fancied too that I could hear breathing – or rather panting. There was absolutely no doubt in my mind that I was being pursued by something that was beyond my ability to identify. My only chance seemed to try to turn the frightening darkness into an advantage by hiding in it. It crossed my mind then that perhaps my pursuer could see in the dark – at least better than I, and if that were so, nothing could help me. But I had no other plan and if I let my brain give way to panic and fear, no hope either.

I remembered that somewhere on my left would be a tall, barred, farm gate that led to the village allotments – at least a dozen plots with all sorts of plants and vegetables and to each a garden shed. In my panic, it occurred to me that if I found a shed, I could somehow evade my pursuer, get inside and secure the door. Even as I was thinking this, the vague, hardly perceptible outline of the gate came up on my left. With an agility born out of fear, I leapt the bars and in spite of catching my foot on the top rail, managed to land upright on the soft ground beyond and ran on into the depths of the allotments.

After only a few seconds, I heard the rattle of the gate as whatever was chasing me climbed over it. In sheer desperation, I stared into the thick darkness before me, seeking any vague outline that might be a garden shed. A solid wall of blackness stared back. Conscious of the noise of the gate, I knew that I had to move fast and change direction as often as possible. I took off to the left, running blindly with my arms outstretched. Within seconds, I crashed into what seemed to be a shrub, soft and yielding and at least as tall as myself. My momentum was such that I penetrated deeply into whatever plant was in front of me and that seemed to be as deep as it was tall. My outstretched hands, and then my face, came into contact with what I thought were hard, woody stems but that I realised seconds later were poles, and some sort of dangling vegetable touched my face. When I tried to stand straight, I found that the poles were fastened together at the top and it became obvious that I had crashed into a thick row of runner bean plants in full growth. I could feel and smell foliage all around me and began to consider that such concealment could be more effective than an uncertain groping around for a shed – a shed that would almost certainly be locked. Perhaps I should stay where I was.

Hardly daring to breathe, I remained absolutely still, reasoning that if I could not see even the plants around me,

I could not be visible to anyone or anything else. After a few seconds, the rushing in my ears from the blood pounding in my head lessened and I concentrated on listening.

There was absolute silence and yet... and yet... I knew, somehow, that something was near and drawing silently closer. Ridiculously concealed in a tepee of beanpoles surrounded by dense foliage, I was too petrified to find anything amusing in the situation.

As the seconds dragged by, I felt a shiver creep up my spine; something was in that blackness that concealed me and though I could neither hear nor see it, I sensed it was very close. Gritting my teeth, I tried to stay absolutely still, held my breath and kept telling myself that my heart pounding in my chest could not possibly be heard outside of my own head. I dreaded the sound of any approaching car in the nearby lane, fearing that even a split-second sweep of headlamps would give away my hiding place.

The seconds dragged by and I dared to hope that I was undiscovered and that my stalker had at last given up and left the scene. Suddenly, there was a sniff; I felt the foliage directly in front of me move, almost imperceptibly. A cold, light touch at the tip of my nose spread across my face until icy fingers slid slowly down my cheeks.

I have seen small creatures die of fright and really felt that I would do the same. My blood ran cold and I ceased breathing as my knees began to buckle and shock deprived me of the slightest movement. A silent scream from my paralysed throat seemed to coincide with the earth beneath my feet beginning to rock. The leaves parted again and a cold face was thrust against mine. I flinched back and, just as I felt consciousness ebbing away, a voice said: 'Jacques?'

And with that husky voice came the musky fragrance that I knew so well.

'Manon?' I stuttered hoarsely.

'Forgive my curiosity, Jacques…' she said in French, '… but what on earth are you doing here among the beanpoles?'

I couldn't see her but the catch in her voice told me she was barely suppressing her amusement.

'Oh, Manon, for Christ's sake, you scared me half to death!' I managed, then catching my breath, 'Why were you chasing me?'

'Chasing you? Why, Jacques, I was just following you, after missing you at the pub. I was just about to catch you up when you suddenly took off like a rabbit. I thought I would find you at the bus shelter. Here, let me pull you out of there… you're shaking like a leaf…'

My terrified state soon began to give way to acute embarrassment and I was grateful that the darkness hid my constant blushing.

Unable to see Manon, I was content to hold her hand and let her lead me to the gate – which she did with seeming ease in spite of the solid darkness. I climbed over the bars on shaking legs and turned to help Manon only to find she had cleared the gate with a jump and was waiting to seize my hand again and lead me to the left, resuming the direction of my walk home.

'Oh my dear Jacques,' she murmured in English, her French accent asserting itself. 'You are still shaking. You should not run so fast after drinking so much of your heavy beer,' she chided.

Her musky perfume hung on the still night air and I clung to her hand like a child to its mother, ashamed of my fear of being separated from her in the darkness.

Very soon, the zebra crossing beacons blinked into view in the blackness and I realised that we were heading for my cottage. Closing with Manon, I put my arm around her slim waist and pulled her to me. She kissed me but then started again towards my home and it was obvious she was determined to walk all the way with me. It was a bit humbling really, being escorted back by a girl. What must she have thought of me, six feet tall, muscular and yet totally dependent on a slim young woman to see me home? It was so excruciatingly embarrassing for me when I thought about it that I began to feign drunkenness as an excuse for my earlier state of panic.

My mind was racing, reliving the time since leaving the pub, trying to analyse what had led me into such a state of fear. It wasn't a physical thing; I would happily defend myself against any man. It really seemed as if my attempts at conquering my phobia of the dark were not effective at all.

I was so engrossed in these thoughts that, before I knew it, we were standing at my gate, although I had not told Manon where I lived. Deftly, as though she could see clearly in the inky darkness, she led me unerringly along the narrow driveway. Not liking to enter a darkened house, I always left a small oil lamp burning just inside the front door so that I could find the keyhole. Manon plunged two fingers into the ticket pocket of my jeans and extracted my key, though how she knew it was there was a mystery. She unlocked the old oak front door and carefully guided me down the single step to the stone floor, leaving me to lean against the wall while she moved into my sitting room and lit the oil lamp there, returned with it to the hall, and then pushed me in front of her into my tiny bathroom. She ran me a hot bath while I sat silent and bemused on the toilet seat. That done, she turned at the door, smiled at me and said, 'I'll be in your bedroom. Don't fall asleep and don't be long.'

Relaxing in the bath, I thought about her familiarity with the geography of my cottage and Lorca's words came instantly to mind: 'Not my business, Mr Jack... but when you have a woman here... I smell her scent sometimes... see her footprints... not yours... too small.'

Was it possible that Manon had been here before? When? How could she get in?

There was so much about my new friend that I did not understand. Was she really following me tonight? It seemed more like a pursuit, almost as if I were being stalked, hunted. Had she seen me with Belle and been angry? Weary of these questions, I thought it really didn't matter: she was in my bed. This stunning-looking, fascinating and mysterious girl was waiting for me...

Ten minutes to finish my bath, brush my teeth and dab on some cologne and I was into the bedroom.

There was no candle or lamp and the room was in total darkness but I sensed she was there on the bed waiting in silence for me to join her. Before I could even call her name, she was on me and with a strength that surprised me, lifted me up and then pinned me down on the bed, sitting astride my chest and pressing down on my shoulders with her cool hands, her long hair falling forward onto my face as I felt her lips on the side of my throat, those big white teeth against my skin. Just for a second, I felt fear, and then her teeth gave way to soft lips again and she kissed me.

Her sensual movements, the fragrance of her hair and the feel of her cool, slim body against mine was the most erotic thing I have ever experienced. She enchanted me and I vaguely remember wondering if, by terrifying me earlier, she had intensified my reactions to her now.

Our love-making that night surpassed even what I had experienced before, in that damp bed in the musty, derelict manor house the previous night, and the mix of strong emotions and exertion from it all led me into a deep, comfortable sleep.

Sunlight through a gap in the curtains woke me. Gradually, the events of the night filtered back into my brain and instinctively I put my arm out for Manon. She was long gone, the bed cold and only the merest outline of her body and lingering, musky perfume revealed that she was ever there. Nor was there any sign of her elsewhere in the cottage.

The elation of having made love with her gave way to the disappointment of her abrupt departure. Again, I wondered if this hot and cold treatment was part of the plan to attract and hold me by keeping me wondering where, when and if I would see her again. If that were so, it was very effective because I could not get her far from my thoughts all through the day.

I couldn't concentrate on anything and wandered in and out of the garden aimlessly. I did some weeding, raking and grass cutting but was unable to settle on anything and found myself regretting that it wasn't Lorca's day to clean so that I'd have someone to chat to and stop obsessing about Manon for a little while.

She was really getting to me. Her method of courtship was about as weird as it gets and yet that was the attraction of it. I had no idea what to make of it other than that I had never been so enchanted by a woman before. There was an edge to it that was something between desire and fear. Yes, that was it… fear. I was just a little bit scared of her – enchanted and afraid.

After lunch, I took to walking in the lane. I told myself that I fancied a stroll but I knew that, deep down, I wanted to see Manon and hoped, quite illogically, that I might bump into her. I was tempted to walk down to the manor house but I couldn't think of any excuse to seek her out and felt instinctively that it would be a mistake to do so. Anyway, she seemed so different on the one occasion I met her during the daytime – shy, reserved, even a bit awkward. She was definitely nocturnal. It seemed an odd coincidence that I should be studying 'darkness' when she was such a creature of the night. I wondered whether, deep in our subconscious and unknown to us, there are connecting lines – links that extend to others through some universal font of knowledge.

Chapter 5

The folded note was on the floor in front of me when I
opened the door. It must have been pushed through the
tiny letterbox while I was out or, more likely, in the early hours
of the morning. There was no envelope, just the folded sheet of
paper. The writing, in black ink, was unusual – a sort of cross
between italic and gothic with the odd flourish that you might
learn on a calligraphy course, the letters big and bold. It was a
summons from Manon to go to the manor that evening. There
was no explanation, no details, not even a time, but that didn't
matter to me. I just wanted to see her, be with her.

Waiting out the afternoon was purgatory and I set off earlier
than necessary. I know it sounds ridiculous but I savoured every
step that brought me closer to her.

In spite of myself, I felt my walking speed increase as I came
nearer to the old front door of the manor. She appeared just as I
went to push it open, as if she had been watching for me, took
my hand and led me down the long, gloomy passageway to a
room on the left at the end. It appeared to be a sitting room
with armchairs and an old chaise longue; French windows
faced the rear garden but were overgrown with shrubs and

provided only a muted, greenish light. Darkness seemed always to accompany Manon.

She kissed me as we entered the room and pointed to the chaise longue. I felt a twinge of disappointment when, instead of sitting beside me, she chose an armchair facing me.

She seemed serious and pre-occupied and I began to think that this was not a romantic 'tryst' as the others had been. She poured me red wine from a dusty bottle with a label mottled with dampness, and took some water herself. Restless and ill at ease, she seemed unable to meet my eyes and I guessed something unpleasant might be about to happen. She took a deep breath and began softly: 'When I first met you, Jacques – I will be frank – it was just a diversion, a chance to flirt with someone who seemed quite different from the locals here. As it turned out, I realised we have French and Paris in common. I like you. The sex is good.'

She paused and stared at the floor. I felt sure that I was about to get the verbal equivalent of a 'Dear John' letter. She looked up suddenly and resumed. 'But now, I realise there is much more to our relationship. I want... I would like, to take things further... for it to be a real romance... with a happy ending – that we live together, happily ever after.'

She forced a smile.

'I'm going to make a proposition to you, Jacques, but first I need to be totally frank with you, to tell you the facts, the truth about me. Only then will you be in the position to make a decision.'

My heart leapt! Not only was I *not* getting the brush off but, quite the contrary, it seemed I was about to be asked to make things serious.

She seemed still to be uneasy, as I had never seen her before. She sipped some more water and began: 'I am now going to take the greatest risk of my life by entrusting you with our...

my secret. It is quite a long story and I ask of you only two things: the first is that you suspend your belief until the end of the story, and the second, that you do not interrupt me until it is finished. You will certainly have many questions and I shall try to answer them. If I fail, if I have misjudged you, it will spell disaster for me and could change my life.'

A tear ran down her cheek and she took a deep breath.

'My father was too young to be called up at the beginning of the war in 1939 and by the time he became of age, he had already entered the police in London. Because of his education, he was quickly promoted and became one of the youngest inspectors of the time. His failure to be able to serve in the war weighed heavily upon him and when, after the surrender, there was a call from the Army of Occupation for men to serve in the various Allied Control Commissions in the occupied zones, he volunteered immediately. He entered the Investigation Branch as a full lieutenant and quickly became a captain. Later, in 1945, he was sent to Austria, to a control point just outside Vienna, which had a Displaced Persons camp attached to it.

'Billeted in a commandeered schloss, my father carried out investigations similar to his work in the London Metropolitan Police but centred on the black market, false papers, drugs, war criminals and a certain amount of espionage. His languages, French and German, served him well and allowed him to foster good working relations with the French Sector. He got on equally well with the US Sector heads but not so much with the Russians.

'Returning one evening from a tiring but successful operation against counterfeiters, he was looking forward to a hot bath and a good dinner. The commanding officer of the British Sector, still suffering from wounds he had received in the war, was on prolonged sick leave and so my father was in overall command with the rank of acting major.

'Before he could indulge in his bath, however, his staff sergeant reported to him and explained that a young woman from the DP camp next door was desperate to see him on an urgent matter, would not be put off and was waiting in his office. Somewhat reluctantly, he agreed, and soon found himself in the company of a shabbily dressed young woman who introduced herself, in French, as a countess from the Hungarian region of Romania. He was immediately taken by what he later described as her "haunting beauty", which transcended her down-at-heel appearance. He had the idea of asking her to dine with him and to tell her story as they ate, thus killing two birds with one stone, so to speak.

'To be brief, my father fell in love during dinner with that mysterious and beautiful aristocrat, just the two of them in the grand dining room of that schloss, lit by candlelight because the power was out, as it frequently was in those immediate post-war days. Everything about her, her striking beauty, her husky voice, her exotic foreign accent and regal manner, bewitched him – an enchantment that would last for thirty years and end only on his death, a few months ago. She seemed to feel the same about him but her troubles weighed heavily upon her and soon the conversation turned to her current crisis.

'She was, she said, the daughter of a Hungarian count and an equally renowned Romanian lady and had enjoyed a privileged upbringing and education. With the outbreak of war, this happy existence changed and the family, particularly her father, were persecuted wherever they went. Her mother died and she and her father became refugees.

'When the Russians invaded at the end of 1943, they were both arrested. Her father subsequently escaped and went into hiding, his whereabouts unknown even to her. She had suffered at the hands of Russian soldiers until she herself escaped and reached the British Zone. This, however, did not ensure her safety as the Russians were demanding her extradition. One particular control officer in the Russian Zone was conspiring to have her arrested and handed over to him personally. This man, she said, had raped her previously and she would kill herself rather than be returned to his custody.

'My father, an absolute gentleman, was immediately moved by this story and tried desperately to console this damsel in distress. By the end of the evening, he was totally bewitched by this beautiful woman whom he called Countess Maria Zaleska to conceal her true identity. Whether she slept with him that first night or at what point they became lovers my mother never told me, but in a very short time they became inseparable insofar as my father's duties allowed.

'This happy state of affairs was soon disrupted by the appearance of the Russian officer who demanded that Eloïse (her real name) be handed over to his jurisdiction. When my father refused him, the officer became threatening and had to be escorted from the schloss by my father's men, at gunpoint. He did not, however, give up and bombarded the British Control High Command with constant written demands of an increasingly threatening tone. Eloïse was terrified of him and held him responsible for the initial hounding of her family and its subsequent break up. Over the next few weeks, the threats became so great that she had to be isolated in my father's quarters and had her own armed sentry.

'In his role as acting chief of section, my father was at first able to refuse all the Russian's demands but later it went over my father's head to the divisional headquarters. There, in spite of my father's pleadings, the senior officer, seeking what he called a "quiet life", granted the Russian application. Both my father and Eloïse were devastated and felt sure that the real motivation behind the demands was the lustful intent of the loathsome Russian major, who was really a political komissar.

'My father was prepared to go to any lengths to save the love of his life even if it were to cost him his career. The two of them made plans to run away together. My father was ideally situated to supply authentic looking false identity documents for Eloïse and, as the day she was to be handed over to the Russians approached, they prepared to flee.'

Manon paused, took a sip of water and studied me as if to make sure that I was listening. Apparently satisfied, she continued: 'As with most plans, Jack, even those meticulously laid, there was room for error and this came in the form of the Russian major foreseeing their intentions. He kept a watch on the schloss and, in the middle of the night chosen by my father for their escape, lay in wait for them both at a deserted section of the road he knew they must take. What happened next was never discussed with me in any detail. It seems certain that there was a fight and that the Russian was killed.

'For many years, I assumed that he died by my father's hand but what I subsequently learned about my mother casts doubt on that. It seems that she was more than capable of killing him herself.

'Anyway, the Russian was hastily buried and the couple escaped Austria. They took a circuitous route, staying in many European countries and taking advantage of those chaotic post-war times when the continent was awash with refugees and displaced persons, carrying all sorts of virtually unverifiable documents.

'Eventually, they settled in Paris. Both the countess and my father were fluent in French and, using the new identities that my father had himself supplied, were subsequently married. We then moved to England and lived here ever since. My father... died a few months ago.'

She got up and opened a second bottle of wine, pouring me another glass. Feeling that I should acknowledge the fact that she had entrusted me with this confidential information, I said: 'Well, Manon, that was all so long ago. You must feel safe now and your father is… er, beyond the reach of any sort of official retribution. I don't understand why telling me could "spell disaster" for you or ruin your life?'

She sat down across from me and leaned closer and I guessed there was more to come and that she was just getting to the really serious stuff, though I couldn't imagine what that might be. She sighed.

'What I shall tell you now, Jacques, is something that you will find very difficult to comprehend and perhaps impossible to believe. I beg you to keep an open mind and would remind you that you have promised not to interrupt. Your questions – and there will be many – I shall try to answer at the end. OK?'

I nodded, wondering what could possibly be coming next that she felt the need to repeat such a grave warning. She drank some more water and took a deep breath. Her anxiety showed in her face.

'How's your biology, Jacques?' She forced a sad smile.

'Less than average, I would think…' I replied with honesty.

'OK,' she replied. 'Let me put it to you in another way. Do you believe that things exist that are, for many reasons, not acknowledged by those who govern us?'

'For example?'

'Well, Jack, do you believe that so-called "authorities" sometimes cover up facts that could be divisive and unsettling to the majority?'

There, she was on safer ground for me.

'Of course I do. I've seen it happen. They don't trouble us with the truth if they deem it disturbing.'

'Yes, "disturbing".' She pounced on the word. 'Yes, that's exactly it.'

I watched her, waiting to see what this introduction was going to bring forth.

'Well, Jack, contrary to what "they" would have us believe, we share this planet with other versions of humanity. Very grudgingly, scientists are having to acknowledge that other types of hominids have lived here. We know now that the Neanderthals did not disappear – that their genes are present in all of us. Darwin coined the phrase "survival of the fittest". Now, think about this: what if, a thousand years ago, humanity was stricken with a virus, let us call it "retrovirus", so deadly that many died but a few, by biological chance, survived the virus and learned to adapt to and live with its symptoms?' She didn't wait for me to reply. 'And as well as symptoms detrimental to health, there were symptoms that were beneficial... no, that's the wrong word... side effects that were beneficial. Are you with me so far?'

I nodded. It seemed logical enough.

'Now we know, Jack, from everyday life, that people deemed "different" from the generally accepted norm are subject to prejudice – sometimes the prejudice of pure ignorance – and what if these "alternative" humans learned very quickly how to hide and disguise those differences so as to be able to exist alongside the common masses of so-called "normal" humans? But you understand, Jack, how very difficult it is to fight superstition and suspicion or just plain ignorance. Religion has a lot to answer for in creating superstition and often condemns those who do not conform to its beliefs, as "spawn of the devil" or "Antichrist". Being different is not classed as a crime but it might as well be!'

She paused to calm down. I had never seen her show much emotion before and was aching to know where all this was leading, while keeping my promise not to interrupt.

'Well,' she said at last, 'my maternal grandfather was one of those who were "different"; one of those who carried the virus and that had been passed down in his family for generations. As if this was not difficult enough for him, he committed the cardinal sin of those of his kind: he dared to fall in love with a *human*! My grandmother, like the vast majority of the human race, was not a carrier of this retrovirus. She was, it might be put, "normal". The couple were ostracised by both of their families and forced to leave the area. Normally – again that loathsome word – the offspring of such a union would not survive birth but on this occasion the female's genes dominated the worst strains of my grandfather's virus and a healthy child was born – Eloïse. Now perhaps you will understand my father's macabre joke in calling Eloïse "Countess Zaleska". Marya Zaleska was allegedly the daughter of Count Dracula!'

She paused to watch as her words slowly filtered through my dumb brain. Dracula? Slowly it seeped through to me – *vampirism*! She was telling me that Eloïse shared her human genes with the genes of her non-human father. I just stared at her as she registered the fact that the 'penny had dropped', at last, in my humble brain. It was all so preposterous that I couldn't think of anything to say, so she continued: 'Look, what this means, Jack, is that I have in my inheritance a certain amount of genes that are "non-human" if you use the definition of "human" accepted today. That is not, of course, without its effect on me but I really hope you will not see me as some sort of hybrid monster.'

She got up and poured me some more wine while I tried desperately to get some sort of control over my racing thoughts.

'I'm nearly finished, Jack. Just try to be patient with me a little while longer. Scientists who recently discovered the Neanderthal DNA in modern humans also discovered genes of as yet unknown origins – so they have known about this and about the changes wrought by the retrovirus for many years but it has been played down. There is already too much prejudice in the world. Now, before you ask your questions, let me assure you that you cannot "catch" anything from me. Mutated genes can be inherited but not passed on in any other way and certainly not by contact. You must understand now how devastating it would be to my life if you revealed my "condition" to anyone.'

My brain felt overwhelmed by what I had just been told. It seemed to go against everything I had ever been taught, yet, in a strange way, it seemed logical.

Seemingly exhausted by her long story, Manon waited patiently to answer the questions she anticipated from me. In truth, I hardly knew where to begin. At last, my brain clearing, I managed to ask: 'And your mother, Eloïse, how badly was she affected…?' I suddenly realised that 'badly' was not a good word and added quickly, 'Or rather in what way was she different?'

She hesitated and I realised how uncomfortable this must be for her.

'Well… well, there were some physical effects but by far the worst was the mental trauma she suffered from having her family hunted down and constantly persecuted wherever they went. You see, Jack, that was the real reason the Russians wanted Eloïse: they had heard from the Hungarian and Romanian villagers that her family were "strigoi", that's their peasant word for vampire, and they wanted her for research. I also believe that the Russian whom my father Peter killed had raped her – at least, that's what *he* believed.'

She got up and came to stand in front of me.

'Look at me, Jack! Do I look like a monster to you? Do you think me a "hybrid", a vampire, or even that such things exist?'

I had never seen her so serious and my heart went out to her. A more beautiful woman it would be hard to imagine and I told her that if she thought that because some of her genes were different from the norm, I would see her as some sort of biological freak, she was quite wrong.

Manon seemed relieved at having unburdened her secrets and possibly unaware of the huge responsibility she had placed on me. Quite how I was expected to behave now was beyond me but I sensed that she wanted to give me a chance to take it all in and that she was expecting me to take my leave of her. I got a real kiss when I left, instead of the friendly 'peck' she had greeted me with.

'Please think carefully about what I have told you, Jack. I know how hard it must be to take in but it's all verifiable fact no matter how fantastic it sounds. Take your time over it all. There is one other very important matter but it will keep. One step at a time. I'll meet you later at the pub.'

She gave me a look that I interpreted as suggesting that our relationship would deepen when this hurdle was surmounted. At the door, she embraced me again and stood watching as I wandered down the drive towards the lane.

It was dark now but I hardly gave it a thought or, for that matter, the progress I was making. With my mind churning and my head aching, I stumbled along between the rows of shrubs and tall trees. Finally, I decided that my best course of action was to head straight for the pub and sink a few pints.

The main road was just a few yards away when I realised that I was not alone. Someone or something was walking stealthily behind me. I called out, 'Who's there?' but there was no answer. I stepped into the lane, turned towards the pub and started running. I didn't stop till I reached the front door. Stupid, I know.

I stayed quite late at the pub but Manon did not appear. I don't know whether I was disappointed or relieved. She had told me so much it was difficult to take it all in and I needed some time to mull it over.

As I left, I saw Belle, smoking outside the back door. I didn't want to talk to her. She seemed always to be fishing for information. She was worse than some of the psychiatrists I've had. She probably meant well but to call her 'eccentric' would be a kind way of putting it; not that I wanted to be a hypocrite.

The night was a bit brighter. The moon and stars were out, all good things, and as well as lighting my way, they gave my spirits a lift. It's hard to worry about the concerns of this world when the vastness of a timeless universe stretches away over your head. It always strikes me as odd that so many people fail to notice that and seem totally preoccupied with trivia instead of being awestruck by the sheer breath-taking beauty of it.

Inevitably, I fell to thinking about the things that Manon had told me. All that business about non-human genes was logical enough the way she explained it but I was not sure that I believed it – although it would be an odd thing to make up and she obviously believed it herself. But then, Belle believed in fairies and thought she was a witch!

If Manon's mother, Eloïse, and her father, Peter, really did kill a Russian officer in 1945, it was all too long ago to be of any consequence now and, anyway, both parents were out of the reach of any sort of belated justice.

By the time I came parallel to the track from the lane to the manor, my spirits were considerably lifted. It was probably the effects of the beer that made me suddenly decide to go there. If Manon would not come to me, I would go to her. My befuddled reasoning told me it would be a good idea: it would reassure her that I had not been scared off by her earlier revelations and, perhaps uppermost in my mind, could lead to spending the night in her bed!

The manor looked welcoming in the moonlight but that welcome was left at the door, since the hallway was pitch black and smelled as damp and musty as I remembered it the night of the storm. I should have been scared again but I suppose the alcohol prevented that.

She must have heard me arrive because Manon was suddenly there, beside me, whispering in my ear. 'I made you come to me, Jacques!'

She took my arm and unerringly led me through the darkness, up the stairs and along to her bedroom – though an odd sort of bedroom it was. There was a dim light from a small bedside oil lamp. Thick curtains covered the only window. There was a double bed with only one cover, a chair, and that was all. It was more like a prison cell than a cosy love nest. I supposed that she had her real bedroom over in the 'inhabited' wing of the house.

Without a word, she pulled me down beside her on the bed and began to remove my shirt. To my delight, in spite of the beer, I responded immediately, such was the attraction of this girl. How could I describe to someone else the enchantment of this woman? Tall, extremely slim, a triangular face with the biggest, darkest eyes I have ever seen, generous mouth with big teeth, very white, and full lips. Her face was framed by long black hair, thick and loose and reaching almost to her waist, long arms and fingers, very white skin, and always that musky scent. In truth, I had never encountered such a woman in all my thirty years and knew that I never would again.

'I thought you said we needed to talk,' I whispered in her ear as she leaned over me. Her mouth on mine ended the conversation. Nothing further could be said until we finished our love-making. 'Love-making' is a quaint term. It really didn't apply to what took place. I felt almost as though I had been raped and I would not have changed it for the world.

'So, Jacques,' she whispered. I loved the way she pronounced my name. 'Do you still want to talk?'

I noticed that she was speaking in French. I loved it.

'What we discussed. What I told you – revealed to you. There is no going back now. It's either trust you or kill you!'

Before I could react to that, I felt her big white teeth against my throat and, for a moment, I was afraid and tensed with fear. She noticed of course.

'Hey, hey, Jacques…!' she whispered. 'I was only joking! Why would I kill the best performing boyfriend I've ever had?'

She sat up and giggled.

When I woke up the next morning, I was quite alone. The bed was cold, Manon long gone. Nor did I find anyone in the house; even the so-called 'residential' wing seemed empty and as I left to go home, I had the sinister but amusing thought that my 'vampire' could be hanging upside down in some dark cellar!

Back at the cottage, Lorca had surpassed herself in cleaning the place and washing my clothes. She was ironing when I came in and eyed me suspiciously, standing over me as I drank the coffee she had already made for herself but shared with me.

She was so good to me in many ways and I felt lucky to have her although she seemed to have appointed herself as a sort of guardian and had an annoying way of making me feel that I needed to explain my movements to her. It was not as if she openly questioned me but interrogated me with her looks. Now, as I slowly sipped my coffee, she didn't take her eyes off my face and I just knew that she was awaiting an explanation as to why my bed had not been slept in. It was, after all, none of her damn business and I was surprised that I felt a bit intimidated by her. It made me even more determined not to give in to her curiosity – in fact, 'nosiness' would have been a better word.

'So, Mister Jack, you looking very tired. You have late night, I think…' she probed, with her approximate English.

'Yes.' I knew a short answer would annoy her. She did not ask again but I could almost feel the frustration as she huffed and puffed. Deliberately, I ignored her and began to read the newspaper I had bought on the way home. Eventually, not having found a way to broach the subject again, she moved out of the kitchen into my tiny sitting room and I could hear her slamming the ornaments down as she dusted.

When Lorca had finished and gone off, barely shouting goodbye, I went into the garden and started some ground clearance that was well overdue and that gave me the opportunity to go over all the stuff that was buzzing in my head. It was difficult to know where to start and I tried desperately to get an edge on it so that I might reason it out piece by piece. I had been given too much information too quickly and needed to break it down into manageable lumps. Some of it, though a total surprise, I could handle. I mean, the story about Eloïse and Peter seemed historically possible. Much more difficult was all that stuff about genes and alternative species of hominids. It was quite beyond anything I had ever heard about before. The facts though did seem to speak for themselves; there was definitely something quite different about Manon and her explanation was the only one I could think of that fitted the facts. It *did* make sense – of a sort.

Stopping for a short rest, I sat on a tree stump and drank a beer. For all that Lorca had been annoyed with me, she was still good-hearted enough to have left a pile of cheese and pickle sandwiches for my lunch. I'd need an evening dinner though; my upbringing in Paris had taught me a love of good food. I'd never learned to cook and decided to splash out on a meal at the pub – hardly cordon bleu of course but not bad. They didn't cook there but took deliveries from a restaurant in the nearest town. If I'd been honest with myself, I would have admitted that it was also a good excuse for a few pints. Alcohol, it is true, had replaced the medication but I considered it much more fun than the tablets, with fewer side effects, and it seemed to do the trick. Better a bottle in front of me than a frontal lobotomy!

It was disappointing to see the pub so quiet but then some local musicians arrived and brought some hangers-on with them. The food was good and, during a break in the music, I went outside for a walk around the beer garden, again refusing to admit to myself that I hoped Manon would be there. This time, I was not disappointed. There, right at the back where the darkest tables stood, was the just visible silhouette of the woman of my life.

When I came closer, I could see that she was smiling at me and my heart beat harder as I saw how stunningly beautiful she looked, her long black hair framing her pale face and seeming to etch her softly into the surrounding darkness. Her white teeth reflected what little light there was and she kept them slightly clenched when she smiled.

'Good evening, Jack.'

She continued to smile at me as she put out her hand to clasp mine as I sat down facing her.

'A beer, or something else? Wine perhaps?' I asked, for the

sake of something to say. She had never accepted anything before.

'I would love to drink wine with you, Jack, especially champagne, but it doesn't suit my digestion. I'm fine.'

So there would never be any chance to get her drunk, I thought, idly. We were quite alone in the beer garden with only the muted strains of music reaching us from the bar, faint and intermittent.

'So, have you considered my proposal about moving in together?' She came straight to the point.

I don't know why but I felt strangely reluctant, still, to commit myself but I realised that she would not be satisfied by more prevarication. Before I could reply, she must have sensed my hesitation because, leaning close, she whispered, 'What makes you so reluctant? Are you afraid of me?'

I took a deep breath and answered, as gently as I could. 'Well... not afraid, exactly... I suppose "wary" would be a better word.'

Before she could reply, I put my hand up to urge her to remain silent.

'Look, Manon, try to see things from my point of view. You have to admit that you have pulled a few scary strokes on me. I mean, following me from the pub one night, stalking me, chasing me into the allotments and scaring me half to death in the dark...'

'*Stalking* you! I merely followed you from the pub... I didn't *chase* you into the allotments... you went in and I followed...'

'Please, Manon, let me finish. Then there's that business of following me home one night and looking through the windows of my cottage and... well... my cleaning lady, Lorca, reckons you've been in my house... at least on a couple of occasions, when I've been out...'

She put her cold hand on my arm and said urgently, 'Wait!

Wait! What are you saying, Jacques, that you find my attentions unwelcome? That my methods of courtship displease you?'

Even in the dim light, I could see that she was giving me a hard look and that she was as close to being annoyed as I had ever seen her – a cold, hard, controlled anger. To try to defuse the situation, I put my hands up, palms towards her and said, '*Doucement, doucement, on se calme!* (Take it easy, calm down!)'

She went quiet then but probably only because a few people were looking in our direction, perhaps, I thought, because we were speaking French rather than any indication of anger on her part.

Refusing another offer of a drink, she sank back a little further into the dark behind our table and sighed. I went for another pint and when I came back she seemed to have recovered her composure and was sitting quietly with a half smile on her face. I took a long swallow of beer and didn't know what to say. I still hadn't answered her question about moving in. I wanted so much to be with her but could not shake the feeling of unease about it.

As we sat looking at each other, a sudden breeze wafted her musky scent towards me and, at the same moment, she tossed her hair out of her eyes. This innocent gesture aroused me instantly and I was amazed that she had such power over me, unlike any woman I had ever known. I saw then that this was my real fear, the reason I was afraid of her: the fear that she could control me, utterly. I had to handle this situation sensibly and not make the mistakes of the past. What an irony that I should have sought out this isolated village and moved here to live an uncomplicated, peaceful life in a simple cottage in order to escape the circumstances and consequences of the 'Event' only to fall into this no-win situation that I just knew would cause me more conflict than ever before. It may have been the beer talking or it may have been some subconscious desire to head off an awkward situation I sensed was coming, I don't know, but I heard myself saying: 'Manon, I want to be frank with you.'

Quite what I wanted to be frank about had not, at that moment, become clear in my mind but failure to act had been my problem in the past and I felt instinctively that I needed to do something now.

'Manon, you seem to think that the main problem with any relationship we might... er... develop is this business about viruses, non-human genes and so forth. But that's not it at all. I don't care about differences, behavioural peculiarities or physiological differences, even if I thought I understood it. The fact is that I've fallen in love with you...'

'So it's not just the sex then?' She laughed.

'Of course it's the sex... that's all part of the falling in love package... but there are other important things as well...'

'What *other* things, Jacques?' she asked, obviously intrigued, a smile hovering on her face. I was embarrassed.

'Well, I don't know... the way you look, the way you dress, the way you are with me...'

She burst out laughing at my discomfort.

'So it *is* just the sex then; that's what you are interested in...'

She probably meant it as a tease but for some reason I felt angry. It flared in me suddenly and I didn't understand why. It seemed to amuse her and she seemed to want to provoke me further.

'*Pauvre Jacques*. I've not been kind to you, have I? You thought you'd found the woman of your life and instead you get the monster from hell!' She burst out laughing again, so loud that I was sure the others in the pub could hear it.

Jumping up so suddenly that I spilled the last of my beer, I stormed out of the beer garden, rounded the pub and set off for home along the dark lane. With every step I took, my anger increased. Instead of a beautiful romance, it seemed I was being used as the butt in some complicated comedy game and now shown to be a complete fool. The thought that I was walking away from the only person I felt I loved occurred to me but my rising anger overcame it and I strode out with a will, believing that I was doing the right thing, however painful the consequences.

I don't know whether subconsciously I was hoping she would run after me but when I stopped to listen, there was no sound of footsteps in the dark lane behind me. Before I knew it, I was level with the path that led to the manor. As I went to pass it, I was hit by something moving so fast that it sent me sprawling into the pathway and I landed with such force that all the air was knocked out of me.

My first thoughts, vague though they were, were that I had collided with a galloping horse and I just lay on the grass as the dew soaked my clothes.

Suddenly, I was hauled to my feet by the back of my shirt and held upright until I had regained my balance. Manon's husky voice whispered in my ear: '*Sois sage, Jacques, tu viens avec moi.* (Be a good boy, Jack, you are coming with me.)'

My arm was held in a strong grip and I was hauled along quickly in the direction of the manor with no time to catch my breath. Unable to speak through lack of oxygen, I had scarcely recovered by the time we reached the door. It was again the deserted wing of the house and, as always, pitch dark. With incredible strength, my 'attacker', who was obviously Manon, dragged me upstairs. I stumbled at the top and was pulled along in the dark with my feet trailing behind me. Although I could see nothing, I was conscious that we had entered a room and a few moments later I was picked up from my knees and thrown onto a bed. Hardly had I landed than she was on top of me tearing at my clothes and meeting no resistance whatsoever from me because my fear was replaced by my realisation that I felt incredibly turned on.

Now that I could breathe again, my body responded automatically to what Manon was doing and soon I was able to take the initiative myself. What followed exhausted both of us and, very ungallantly, I must have fallen asleep.

Light pouring through a window where the curtain rail had collapsed eventually woke me. The space in the bed beside me was empty and cold and, after dressing and going downstairs, I found the house was too, prompting again silly and unkind visions of Manon hanging upside down in some dark cellar like a giant vampire bat!

There seemed nothing to do but go home and it was then, as I walked back, that I realised how bruised and battered I was. My ribs hurt and my back ached and I was surprised to find a painful swelling on my cheek bone where I had initially been knocked down. By the time I reached the cottage, I was one big ache, very tired, and my earlier elation had given place to a moroseness verging on depression.

Lorca greeted me with obvious dismay and, receiving no answers to her barrage of questions, slunk off to run me a very hot bath, presenting me with a cup of tea before I got into the tub.

I soaked in that bath until the water went cold, my mind churning on the events of the evening before. In reality, I had been attacked, assaulted and dragged off to be raped – at least it would have been rape if I had not so readily consented! And in the morning, nothing. Not even a 'goodbye'. Lorca's grudging but natural kindness seemed almost compassionate in comparison and I wondered why I was unable to lavish my misguided affections on her.

When I finally emerged, Lorca was still there, though it was well past her leaving time and I felt she had stayed to check on my well-being but, compassionate or not, she did not feel disposed to being very sympathetic. It was obvious that she was seething to find out what had happened to me. Maybe, with the bruises visible, she thought that I had been in a fight. Finally, she could no longer hold in her curiosity.

'Mr Jack, what are these shenanigans?' She pronounced the word all wrong and I guessed it was something she had recently picked up. Of course, the last thing I wanted was to be interrogated by her but, remembering her little gestures of kindness and her apparently genuine interest in my well-being, I tried not to be short with her.

'Shenanigans, eh, Lorca? That's a good word.'

'Mr Jack, I concerned for you, sometimes often now. Perhaps if you drank less beer…'

'You're right, Lorca. I need to cut down on alcohol. I'll try, I promise.'

She looked me up and down and heaved a long sigh. Kind and well-meaning as she was, I was longing for her to leave. I couldn't concentrate on anything when she was around and I needed now to do some serious thinking. What had happened to me the night before was tantamount to an assault, an act of aggression that, though it led to passionate love-making, took my relationship with Manon to a whole new level. Frankly, I was scared. I had never been attacked by a woman before and the sheer violence of it surprised me. Of course she was angry. I'd childishly walked away and left her without a word of goodbye. It was rude and unpardonably impolite and, I hoped, entirely out of character. Probably, I should have turned around, walked back to the beer garden and apologised. Instead, I didn't get the chance. If she had run after me, called me a rude sod and even slapped my face, I would not have blamed her in the least but that she was capable of such violence, possessed such strength and was prepared to act the way she did – well, it just shocked me.

At the same time though, I suppose I felt a bit flattered that such a beautiful and unusual woman would feel so strongly about me that she could act in such a passionate way. There was no disputing that the love-making was just incredible. That I should be the object of such intense desire on her part overwhelmed me. I knew that I was prepared to forgive anything just to be part of her life. Never before had any woman captivated me in that way. But now I didn't know where I was with her. My 'power-play' had backfired on me spectacularly and I was now afraid that I had blown it and our love-making had been her farewell gesture.

The whole thing troubled me so much that, just for a moment, I felt like sharing the turmoil of my thoughts with Lorca – getting a perspective from one who seemed so sensible and down to earth. The more I thought about that, the more I came to thinking that it would not be a good idea; the whole tale sounded too fantastic. And anyway, Lorca was already suspicious of me. It had been she who warned me about the mysterious footprints in the cottage; she who sensed a woman's presence there, other than her own. She knew that something was going on and would probably give me good advice about it but that advice would almost certainly be to stop, to never see Manon again and to avoid her and the manor like the plague. And that was exactly what I couldn't and wouldn't do.

That it would all end in tears was obvious to me but I would not miss it for the world. My life needed some excitement; it needed a radical change. Since the 'Event' I had been stagnant – going through the motions of life, not living, just existing.

The door slamming brought me out of my reverie and I realised that Lorca had just gone and that I'd probably offended her when that was the last thing I'd intended.

Creeping into my tiny sitting room, I put some classical music on the record player, pulled the throw from the sofa over me and curled up into a ball, nursing my bruises. My thoughts lay jumbled in my head but I believed that if I could just get to sleep, I might wake up to find my subconscious had sorted out a plan of action.

BELLE'S DIARY

Monday, 21 July 1971

Saw that Jack guy again tonight, in the pub of course. God! He looked dreadful. It was obvious he didn't want to talk. Had his beer and left. Perhaps it's just as well'cos I'm back on the medication again now and if I'd accepted a drink from him, I'd have been back down that slippery path that got me banned from the place last year.

Can't help wondering, though, what's bugging him. I don't know what powers he possesses or even if he knows he has them but I can definitely see an aura around him. Of course, the others don't see anything. How could they? They're all simple souls really. I don't mean to be derogatory, it's just that being psychic is in my family and it's a gift not bestowed on many. Crystal balls and tarot cards may look impressive but I don't need any of that. It's a mixture of instinct, detailed observation and then that little bit of witchcraft that I've inherited.

This Jack guy was damaged goods when he arrived in this village. It's about the worst place he could have landed up in.

It's his 'familiar', you see – or rather, I see. Someone, another witch perhaps, has cursed him. It's as plain as day to me but I don't know how to get him to talk to me about it. He seems unaware that anything is wrong with him.

I'm seeing Esme next week. I'll ask *her* about it. Exorcisms are more her line of work.

All the same, I feel a catastrophe looming and it's unsettling me.

Sod it! Just one drink won't hurt.

CHAPTER 6

*'There is no exquisite beauty... without some
strangeness in the proportion.'*
EDGAR ALLAN POE, *LIGEIA*

It was, in fact, some time until I saw Manon again. I did not seek her out and, true to my promise to Lorca, I did not visit the pub.

Time passed gently, the daytime in my garden and the evenings in my tiny sitting room, reading by oil lamp. Nor did I consider all the things that Manon had confided in me, knowing from long experience that direct thought never solved any problems for me. I believed it best to let my subconscious mull things over – a variation of the old decision-making system of sleeping on it.

Mentally, I was almost at ease but after four days my physical desire for Manon began to assert itself and she began to feature heavily in my thoughts in general and in my dreams in particular.

It was then midsummer and, although the longest day had passed, it still did not get really dark until quite late. It was almost a week after our last meeting when I decided to seek her out.

Using our usual system, I duly presented myself at the pub and sat confidently at the back of the beer garden. By my third pint, however, Manon had not appeared – if 'appeared' accurately described her furtive presence in the darkness. With more than a little disappointment, I decided to walk home, knowing she was quite able to find me on the darkest of nights. I stopped for one last beer and set off into the darkness towards my cottage.

The lane leading down to the manor was barely discernible in the thick darkness and presented an unattractive prospect, yet I realised suddenly that, with the new knowledge furnished by Manon's revelations, there was no longer any reason to fear since the 'thing' that had been stalking me was she herself and not some frightening entity from the Egyptian *Book of the Dead* that my fervid brain had imagined. Perhaps the beer helped too but I decided, rashly, that I could overcome the instinctive fear of the dark path. The prospect of sleeping with Manon was just too attractive. It seemed odd that I could set so much store by my subconscious decision-making and yet was so easily able to dismiss the warnings of my instincts. I took the manor path.

About a hundred yards along, groping my way in pitch darkness, I began to regret my rashness and decided to turn back but found that it was more easily said than done. The path at that spot, shrouded by tall bushes to the exclusion of the weak starlight, was pitch dark and I was afraid to turn round in case I became completely disorientated and wandered off into the bushes or a ditch. So by putting my feet down tentatively and feeling the flat part of the path, I continued to advance slowly towards the house.

There were no lights on at the manor and the only way I knew I was close was when I walked straight into the old wicket gate at the end of the path. Surmising that I was within twenty yards of the door to the deserted wing of the house where I knew that Manon had a bedroom I held my arms out in front of me and advanced carefully until I touched the old oak door surround and, moving slightly to my right, I extended my arm to where I judged the door should be. At first, I felt nothing but then my hand touched something that, to my horror, moved! I snatched my hand away with an involuntary cry and made to step back. Something gripped my shirt in the middle of my chest and I was jerked forward into the pitch-black hallway. A cool cheek touched mine with a slight noise somewhere between a sniff and a low growl. Frozen with fear, I felt myself go rigid, unable to move. And then, to my huge relief, I smelled that musky perfume exuded by Manon.

'Come in, Jack,' she whispered in my ear. 'I have been expecting you.'

The same musty, damp smell I remembered pervaded the hallway and up the stairs and I wondered what it would be like in winter. Manon ushered – almost dragged me – along the corridor unerringly in complete darkness and into a room lit only by a dark-shaded oil lamp, sat me down and pulled up a chair opposite. By the dim light, I could just make out her beautiful features, her long hair braided and hanging in front of her shoulder.

'How are you, Jacques?' she reverted to French. 'Not too drunk I hope.'

'I was hoping to find you at the pub,' I offered, for the sake of making some sort of answer.

'I knew you would come here, Jacques. I made you come.'

I ignored the attempt to convince me of her special powers and must have sighed because she leapt up and sat on my lap. Turning my head with her hand under my chin, she kissed me – a long, passionate, erotic kiss. Suddenly, she broke away and stood up.

'Enough! You always fall asleep after we make love, so I will talk to you first.'

She sat down again, facing me, and I sensed something serious was coming. For one dreadful moment, I thought she might be about to tell me that she didn't want to see me anymore and I found I was holding my breath.

'Now that you know everything – well almost everything – about me, I want to put my proposition to you again: why don't you come and live here? Leave your little cottage and move in here with me…?'

I gasped with relief. I don't know what I would have done if she'd finished our 'affair'.

'Oh, Manon, you frightened me… I…'

She put her finger on my mouth.

'I am *not* Manon, Jack! Manon does not exist… there is no "Manon", just me, Eloïse.'

I stared at her in total confusion.

'Cheer up, Jacques. I've had enough of deceiving you. Just this last hurdle and things will be a lot less complicated.'

My mind slipped into neutral and I just sat there staring at her, my feeble brain unable to compute what she had just said.

She got up but, within seconds, she was back with a glass for me and a bottle of Armagnac, pouring me a big measure. I sipped the fiery but smooth liquid as I waited for my mind to focus on her words. After a long silence, I managed to say, 'Explain it to me, please. I think I'm in the dark both physically and mentally.'

'Relax, Jack. I will explain it all. Most of what you have been told is true. The English soldier and his "hybrid" countess did fall in love; they did kill the Russian major and they did escape to Paris and lived there happily for many years. But the "hybrid" countess was sterile and could not produce "human" offspring and so they could never have children. He, Peter, died last year, as you already know, and that left me, Eloïse, all alone.'

She paused and seemed to be watching my face. After a while, clearly thinking that I understood, she leaned close and whispered: 'Yes, Jacques, that refugee woman, the "Countess Zaleska", as my husband called her, was me, or rather, *is* me. Manon? I just invented her because I thought you would never be able to believe that a woman alive in 1945 could look as young as I do now. Believe me, Jacques, I am sorry to have deceived you but, the truth is, I'm so lonely since Peter died and I need someone to be with me… to love me, hold me, protect me and look after me. That person, I feel, is you. Please try to understand – all this deceit about "Manon" was with good intention. I know how unbelievable it must all sound to you and I just wanted it to seem less fantastic. I thought that if I pretended to be my own daughter, it would minimise the gene thing; twenty-five per cent non-human doesn't sound as bad… and, anyway, I had to deceive the local people too because I had to deal with them after Peter died and they would have expected me to look as old as he did. Please, Jacques, answer me.'

I think that when the human psyche is faced with overwhelming information that defies all logic, it shuts down, or at least it slows down. When she realised that I was unable to say anything, she took my hand and kissed it, came very close and stared into my eyes as though she was able to read my thoughts.

'Jacques,' she murmured, 'forgive my deceit. I will never deceive you again. Come and live here. We can be happy. I will look after you and you look after me. We can make it work. Peter and I had more than thirty good years. Look at me, Jacques! Do you see an old woman? Do you see a monster? I am old by your years but young by mine. Am I not still beautiful? Come to bed now; I will show you how much I love you.'

She pulled me up and out into the pitch-dark passageway and then along to the bedroom we had shared before. The bed was cold and Eloïse also, but it was not long before our love-making warmed it up. What followed between us was as wonderful as I have described before and, when it finished, ungentlemanly as it may be, I crashed out into a deep sleep.

This time, when I woke up, Eloïse was still with me. She seemed wide awake and I realised that she had probably not been asleep. I watched as she got up, her tall, slim figure silhouetted against the sunlit curtains. She dressed and put on dark glasses before drawing the blinds.

This was the first time that I had seen her in the morning. She looked exactly the same as the night before, not a hair out of place and her huge dark eyes bright behind the dark lenses of her sunglasses. I wondered, idly, how she lived – I'd never seen her eat anything – and I stupidly ran my hand under my chin. I don't know what I expected to find – wounds in my throat, I suppose. She had her back to me but seemed to see my silly gesture and spun round to face me. I expected her to be angry; it was a cretinous thing for me to have done. Instead, she climbed back into bed and coming very close to me, emitted a low growl and then snarled loudly, showing those huge, beautiful teeth! It was so sudden and unexpected that it made me jump and shrink back into the pillow. She burst out laughing.

'Oh, Jacques...' She caught her breath. 'Did you really think I wanted you for a meal? Did you think that I sucked your blood in the night?'

She was convulsed with laughter and it infected me too. We both laughed loud enough to awaken the dead. An unfortunate metaphor, as it turned out.

'You must learn to trust me,' she said, when we had both recovered. 'Jacques, you cannot live a life of fear believing your lover is a monster.'

I felt really stupid and immature and tried to make things right.

'Eloïse, I'm so sorry, but you must see what an extraordinary situation I am in. Your revelations have come as a great shock to me. Even now, I'm not sure I understand it or actually believe it all but, if you are patient with me, I'm sure that I can come to accept it.'

'Of course, Jacques. You are only human, after all!'

And we burst out laughing again.

Sitting in a particularly shady part of the garden, I sipped the coffee that Eloïse had made me, while she, wearing her dark glasses and a sort of dark veil, sipped a glass of water. We both knew that we had a lot of serious decision-making to do but were mutually reluctant to face up to it. I tried hard to imagine what life with Eloïse would be like. It was certain that I was infatuated with her and the sex was fantastic, but could I love her in the real meaning of that word? Life with her at the manor sounded idyllic but we would be totally isolated from everything and everyone. Not needing to go out to work, pottering about at leisure in that huge garden and making love to and being loved by a beautiful woman would be every man's dream – but at what cost?

There would be no friends or guests, no family, and we would forever be looking over our shoulders and keeping this dark, scarcely believable secret. Eventually, I would grow old and Eloïse, it seemed, would not. Would she tire of me and be out at night seeking new blood? Another unfortunate metaphor, under the circumstances.

'By the time that happens, Jacques, you will be too old to

care,' she said, although I had not spoken this thought out loud. Could she read my thoughts? How frightening would that be?

The sun had moved round and now shone directly on to our table. Eloïse shrank back into the shade of a huge, unkempt rhododendron. A little cloud of flies buzzed annoyingly around my head but left her in peace. Perhaps it was my imagination but it seemed that all the birds, squirrels and rabbits that were normally in evidence had deserted us too and I was suddenly aware that my beautiful companion did not fit into the scene; that she really was, somehow, alien to that normal, simple scenario, in a way that I could feel but not explain.

I had so many questions that I didn't know where to begin but the warm sunlight and my exertions of the night increased my drowsiness.

Eloïse seemed content just to sit and observe me and I had the impression that she believed she'd convinced me, as indeed she had.

At last, echoing my most recent thoughts, she said, 'I have money. Lots of it. Peter was a very shrewd investor. We bought this manor outright years ago and there are monies left in trust. We would have no financial cares. As "Manon", I've even been out locally, shopping, when Peter became too ill to do it. So you see, on a worldly basis, we have no problems. But the *spiritual* side of things… that's the difficult part. Are you religious, Jacques? It would be quite difficult for you…'

'I'm not,' I answered her, quickly. 'Nor do I believe in sin. Of course, I have my ideas about right and wrong but that's not anything to do with religion.'

She made no reply at first but then said, at last, 'Do you know that for hundreds of years people like my father – people like me – have been cursed and persecuted by religion? At last, science has confirmed that even so-called modern man has traces of Neanderthal, Denisovan and other hominids in his genes, and yet the persecution and superstition continues. What hypocrisy!'

She sat back and became calm again.

'Do you understand, Jacques, that had evolution taken a slightly different turn, my people would have been the norm and yours would be the "monsters"?'

She laughed, pleased with the thought.

'We have so much more to offer,' she continued, suppressing a giggle. 'We live much longer, we are much stronger and our bodies require little maintenance…'

'And you are beautiful too…' I added, to join in her mood. She became serious again.

'We hybrids are sterile – chimeras, some say,' she mused. 'What a shame, Jacques. We could have had a family of "superkids".'

She became thoughtful again.

'Jacques, please say you'll do it… come and stay here… and love me, if you can.'

Suddenly, she looked so sad, her dark glasses unable to hide the tears that trickled down her cheeks. I knew then what my answer must be and nodded my head. She jumped up and kissed me and hugged me to her. In spite of my foreboding, I felt that I now had the chance to do something decent with my hitherto worthless existence.

All that confusing and mysterious business about 'Manon' was now out of the way. I was still a little peeved with Eloïse for concocting it all and making everything so complicated but I could understand her reasoning. How could I have accepted, at first meeting, that *she* was the woman – the countess – from 1945? It was difficult enough for me to understand it now but a little easier to accept. If I couldn't make that leap of faith and embrace her story, nothing would make any sense at all. An imperfect explanation was better than none, and was it really so fantastic after all? I had learned that, without doubt, I was dealing with an extraordinary person with both physical and mental attributes far in advance of anything I had known before. Once I was able to admit that, her story became much easier to accept. And anyway, what did it matter whether it was actually true if I wanted it to be so? Truth is subjective and her story was true to me or, at any rate, I couldn't prove it false.

I wanted to be with her – it was as simple as that. The truth is not always desirable.

CHAPTER 7

'This thing of darkness I acknowledge mine.'
WILLIAM SHAKESPEARE, *THE TEMPEST*

Moving in with Eloïse proved to be a lot easier than I had imagined. After a great deal of discussion, we had both agreed to an initial one-month stay – a trial period that we thought would be long enough to see how things worked out.

The technicalities were soon completed; I told Lorca that I was leaving the cottage for a month to stay with friends and softened her loss of employment with eight weeks' money and a ticket to Romania to visit her family. She may have been a bit suspicious of my real motives but the chance of a paid holiday in her mother country was too good to quibble over.

I didn't need much in the way of packing since I could easily slip back for anything I might need.

Among the many things that Eloïse and I discussed was, of course, money. She insisted that she would handle anything and everything financial. Her late husband, Peter, had been very successful in the stock market and had left her ample funds. More money, she claimed, than she could spend in twenty-five years. The manor house itself cost little to run: because of her aversion to strong light, she used candles and oil lamps. Indeed, we would cut off the electricity and it would not be a problem for her. There were log-burning stoves and fires and, although she seldom used them herself, they would be available to me, and the woodland of her estate would supply all the fuel we might need. When it came to food, Eloïse ate only small amounts of the simplest sort, mainly vegetables, but said that she would cook 'proper' meals for me using the skills she learned in Paris. Alcohol did not figure at all in her needs but there was a well-stocked cellar. Peter had been a man of some taste and he knew his way around wine. She added that she would not expect me to stop visiting the pub.

We would move into rooms in what she referred to as the 'habitable' wing of the manor. I was to have my own bedroom with carpets and furnishings and where Eloïse would visit when it was 'time for love-making', as she quaintly put it. There was also a fairly modern kitchen, a morning room and a parlour, both furnished in Victorian style. There would be no visitors and no deliveries or callers. The very occasional shopping for basic necessities would be my responsibility as Eloïse disliked being seen.

When all this had been more or less agreed, Eloïse came over and sat down on my lap. The mere touch of her body against mine and her long cool fingers caressing my face was enough to arouse me and her musky scent heightened my desire. Even her odd behaviour attracted me; she could move very quickly, often disappearing and then reappearing seconds later, carrying a drink for me.

She was also immensely strong and could lift and carry loads far in excess of anything that I could manage. It was a disconcerting thought that I would have no chance against her if she ever became violent towards me! She could see in the dark and, although I had no proof of it, I was convinced that she had a heightened sense of smell because she would find me wherever I was in the grounds even if I made no noise at all and was hidden from sight. I would hear her sniffing like a dog.

But it was her mouth and teeth that so much attracted me; though her face tended towards the triangular, the skin very pale and made even paler by her jet-black hair that almost reached her waist, there was room for a sensuous mouth. Her teeth were big and very white and her mouth always tasted so fresh and clean. She had, however, a slightly disconcerting habit of baring her teeth in close proximity to my throat and, on a couple of occasions, had, at the height of passion, seemed to nip my neck and throat very gently. It was at those moments that I had to fight down my fears and tell myself not to let my imagination run away with me. If she hadn't said all that stuff about vampires, it would probably not have worried me.

I was entranced with my 'lady friend', as Eloïse liked to be called. It goes almost without saying that I had never before met anyone remotely like Eloïse and was certain that I never would again. She enchanted and bewitched me and, frankly, I couldn't wait to move in with her and considered myself to be the luckiest man in the world.

The year that followed was the best year of my life. The first week was spent sorting out our pre-agreed roles and making ourselves comfortable, each in our own way, in the habitable part of the manor. Eloïse had thoughtfully stored away all traces of Peter and the life she had shared with him and although I now had his room, there was nothing to remind me that I was anyone other than Eloïse's man.

True to her word, she was kind and considerate towards me, appreciated my differing needs and different lifestyle, and did her best to create for me the cosiness and homeliness that I craved, in spite of it being completely alien to her.

So when the autumn came upon us, she agreed to let me have log fires in the rooms (except her bedroom) and use more oil lamps and candles to brighten our evenings. On one occasion, I confided to her my fascination with the sheer elegance of Victorian ladies and she subsequently surprised me by wearing Victorian dresses and putting her hair up on top of her head in the style of the 1890s. She even told me that she had been born in 1874 and so had grown up in that era but when she could see that I was not inclined to believe that she was as old as my grandfather, she quietly dropped the subject. And yet, to my delight, she appeared again in Victorian dress the following night and was every bit the Victorian lady.

We had fallen into a routine that suited us both. She was largely nocturnal but I didn't mind that at all. I stayed up late with her, slept late in the mornings and used the afternoons to do some work or, very occasionally, some shopping; then I would wash and change to join her when she appeared in late afternoon or early evening.

With neither television nor radio, we read, ate and drank (at least I did) but mainly we talked. An uncomfortable fact it may have been for me, but Eloïse had lived a long, long time and she could tell me from first-hand experience what life was really like during every one of those eras. She had lived all over Europe and was polyglot and multi-cultured. We spoke English sometimes but mainly French, though Eloïse was also fluent in German, Romanian, Hungarian and Russian. She introduced me to the cultures of all those places and, of course, we always had our beloved Paris in common. Eloïse had the culture and knowledge of one hundred years of living and it was a delight to listen to her husky voice with its slight foreign inflexions, describing first-hand historical events that I had only read about in history books. Her exquisite manners, her tasteful elegance and her ability to see into my mind enchanted me and, far from feeling that I was living with an alien, I began to appreciate how lucky I was to be there with her.

The year sped past too quickly and I soon realised that I would do anything she asked of me so that our time together should continue. Nothing disrupted our happiness. No one came and no one went and that was just as we wanted it. Gradually, I learned more about this lovely creature who was sharing this small part of her life with me – little things of no real consequence to her but were fascinating to me: her ability to read my mind to a certain extent; her oneness with nature and her acceptance of the fact that she had been born so different from the vast majority. She did not sleep as I slept but rather seemed to go into a trance that relaxed her mind. She could do this standing up and could remain standing, absolutely motionless, for hours at a time, silent, her eyes open and fixed, staring without blinking, like some sort of mannequin.

She never seemed tired or was moody and although superior to me in every way, physically and mentally, never showed any indication of impatience or condescension towards me – though she did sometimes burst out laughing when I said something stupid. She was then full of remorse at the possibility that she had upset me.

Here and there, I gleaned fragments of her life – or rather, lives, in various countries. I learned more about the persecution of her family, the constant moving from place to place to avoid the prejudice and ignorance of people so obviously racially and intellectually inferior to herself and her family. If she was bitter at the hand that fate had dealt her, she did not show it and spoke with affection for the 'humans' who had helped them down the years. I gathered that I was now one such, the latest in her long life and, of course, though she did not say it, doomed to grow old and leave her eventually.

Nor could I ever forget the love-making that often

followed our wonderful evenings. Eloïse became livelier as the night wore on and would often wake me only a few hours after we'd had sex to ask me to do it all again – something I could never have achieved if I had been obliged to go out to work for a living.

One of the many 'unusual' things about her was that she never seemed any different – by that I mean that she never changed her usual happy disposition, never sulked, never got angry, never quarrelled with me or got aggressive (except occasionally in her love-making).

Physically too, she seemed permanently at her best, never became ill, had a headache or a cold, nor looked as though she was out of sorts, never smelled less than fragrant, had untidy hair, or had a blemish on her complexion.

In fact, life with Eloïse was for me like finding my dream woman and the only negative thing was my concern that things were too good to last. Fortunately, I was able to put this thought to the back of my mind and had the sense to enjoy the moment, to live from day to day (or rather from night to night) and not to reason why. And when, on rare occasions, such concerns got the better of me, I consoled myself by thinking that nothing could destroy the happiness I had already experienced with Eloïse.

Winter finally dissolved into spring and I was kept busy in the gardens and grounds and making repairs to the huge old house. With the milder weather, to vary our activities, we took to long walks around the grounds in the evenings after the sun had lost its power and Eloïse felt comfortable in the subdued light. Strolling in the warm and scented spring air, holding hands, we were perfectly at ease with each other.

Lorca, it seemed, had stayed in Romania and so I let my cottage on a year's lease, the rent money allowing me to feel that I could contribute financially to our life together. Meanwhile, as spring turned to summer, Eloïse had adopted another way of astonishing me with her infinite variety. She turned up for our evening meal in the parlour wearing clothes from a different era each night. Her uniform from World War II was so different from her usual long dresses that I found it difficult to believe it was actually Eloïse.

My life with her was an absolute delight and I missed her even while I waited for her to appear each day in the late afternoon. Her long and varied life made me feel intellectually inferior but Eloïse took great pains to avoid seeming patronising or making me feel ignorant. She seemed to have endless patience, was permanently in good spirits, and I felt proud that I seemed to be as good for her as she was for me.

All my life, I had resented change and found it was invariably change for the worse. So I began to plan and scheme ways to ensure the continuation of the status quo.

Our evenings together were the highlight of my day and I looked forward to them immensely. We always found something interesting to discuss but just being with her would have been enough for me. She would ask about my day just as other couples speak about their work and I felt sometimes that she would have loved to be able to join me during the daylight hours, had that been possible.

One day, poking about in one of the overgrown outbuildings, I found an old motorcycle. Very old, it had the gear change on the square petrol tank, with an oil pump mechanism next to it. Peter must have been a great collector and I guessed that the bike was quite valuable. It took me most of the day to get it going, with fresh oil, grease and bruised fingers. Once I'd flushed out the petrol tank, the mower petrol worked fine and eventually it ticked over sweetly. The brake cables needed unseizing and the perished tyres carefully inflated before a test run up and down one of the flatter fields.

It was great fun and when Eloïse appeared that evening, I told her all about it. To my amazement, she shared my excitement and insisted on having a ride.

It was a soft, warm evening with a nearly full moon, bright enough to see the whole field. I kicked the motor into life and, before I could ask her, Eloïse clambered onto the saddle behind mine.

The old bike revved smoothly although a small hole in the silencer made it sound quite loud, not that there was anyone to hear it. It wobbled about a bit and I worried about our combined weight on the old tyres.

Finally, I was able to get my feet up on to the rests and took us down the field at a respectable rate. Eloïse had her arms around me and I could smell her musky scent and the fragrance of her long hair. Turning at the far end, I gunned the engine hard. The bike took off down the return straight and we both hung on for dear life. Eloïse loved it; I could hear her laughter over the noise of the motor. When we reached the halfway mark, I had the strangest feeling that life was standing still for me, that I was fixed in space and time on this old motorbike with the woman of my life clinging to me as if nothing else mattered and we were suspended from existence.

Eventually, the moon went behind the clouds. The bike's dynamo was not charging and the battery was flat, the lights so dim that it was impossible to continue. Eloïse helped me wheel it back to the outhouse and, grasping my hand, made me run back to the manor. The bike ride seemed to have turned her on because she pushed me down on the carpet and straddled me, pulling off her clothes and mine.

Our love-making was, for me at least, perfect and when we finished and lay back staring at the flickering lamplight on the ceiling, I felt a happiness that I had truly never experienced before. Life, I felt, could never be better and I wondered what I had done to deserve such happiness.

Another day, I repaired the old oak door in the brick wall enclosing what had once been a 'secret garden' and then decided to finish replanting the place as a surprise for Eloïse.

Anticipating her delight, I got so engrossed in clearing and planting that I didn't notice the time passing until it started to get dark and I thought I might be late back to the house for whatever Eloïse might be cooking for me. I didn't realise quite how late it was until I started to trudge back. The lamps were lit in our part of the house but Eloïse was not there and that surprised me a bit as she was usually up at dusk.

I showered and when I came out it was to find a note on top of a neatly folded dark suit. Eloïse's distinctive spidery handwriting jumped off the page at me. Apparently, we were going to have a surprise soirée and I was to change and join her in the old part of the house as soon as I could. This puzzled me because I knew how decrepit everything was over in that wing and unlikely to be the perfect setting for a soirée.

The clothes were an old business suit of mine that Eloïse had deftly altered. Years of making her own clothes and of living through so many fashion changes had given her a certain expertise and the suit fitted me perfectly, though altered to a much earlier style with wide, double-breasted lapels and a more fitted waist.

Feeling a bit self-conscious, I made my way towards the

unused wing of the house and soon its desolation, mustiness and state of semi-dereliction called to mind the night of the storm that I had spent there, frozen in fear. There was also, of course, the very pleasant memory of our first love-making.

Eloïse had left lighted candles along the route and near these were small paper arrows directing me at last to the room behind the main staircase that, when I had first seen it, seemed to be a cross between a sitting room and a library.

This was obviously a special occasion because as I approached the old oak door set in dark and dusty panelling, I could just discern the faint sound of music. The musty smell and dampness stopped at the door of this room. Inside it was warm and welcoming; oil lamps and candelabra were dotted all around, suffusing a soft, warm light in addition to the open fire. The antique furnishings had been pushed to the sides to clear a central space. Somewhere in the background, a wind-up gramophone with a large horn ground out a dance melody, slow and haunting, with accordions, violins and a slow, rhythmic pulse and a lady singer with a sad voice that seemed as if it were coming through the ether from the spirit world, in a Slav language I didn't understand. Eloïse told me later that it was a popular dance tune from Serbia called '*Jutros mi je ruza procvetala*'.

If Eloïse had intended to create in this room a scene of mystery and old-world enchantment, she had certainly succeeded. The soft glow of the oil lamps and the flickering, dancing light from the candles made the whole room look dreamlike. Even the old-fashioned and shabby furnishings looked soft and comfortable and the new warmth seemed to have destroyed the mustiness of this old, disused part of the house, usually shut up and little aired.

Eloïse appeared suddenly at my side in that unsettling way of hers. She did not speak or even look at me and stood next to me so that only her profile was visible. She took my breath away. Her unusual height made her look even slimmer than usual because of a long, black, tight-fitting dress, showing her beautiful figure at its best. Her long, dark mane was swept up on top of her head in a sort of beehive but with a long plait hanging down her back. From the side, her face appeared almost triangular with its prominent cheekbones and heavy, slanting eyebrows – a profile that would have made the perfect silhouette portrait so beloved by the Victorians.

She took my hand and drew me closer, still in silence. She faced me and came into my arms and I realised that I was expected to dance. Holding her tightly, I could smell that beautiful musky fragrance that I had long since recognised, not as a perfume but her own natural scent.

Dancing has never been my thing. I have little sense of rhythm or ease of movement so I just followed her lead and we moved off into what seemed to me to be a very slow waltz. She appeared so light and elegant, holding her head up high as they do in the tango.

I had long since grown accustomed to the coolness of her skin but on that night she seemed to take on the warmth of her surroundings. Moving gently around the room to the strains of this melancholy, haunting refrain, in the presence of this mysterious and enchanting woman, I felt almost detached from life, my life, as I had formerly known it. I wanted to be with her, like that, forever and never allow it to stop. I felt instinctively that I would never know a happier time and I wanted that dance to go on and on ceaselessly.

It felt as though I could never achieve greater happiness and needed to preserve it as you would capture time in a photograph. My overwhelming feeling of contentment must have communicated itself to Eloïse because she pulled me even closer to her and brushed seductively against me as we danced slowly and, of course, alone, around the huge old room.

The dance finished all too soon for me and the gramophone clicked into its end groove. Eloïse broke away and came back with a glass of champagne for me before attending to the next record. The next piece of music, while not as enchanting in melody as the first, was even more hauntingly evocative. It was a weird feeling, just the two of us, moving in a circle like ghosts in a haunted house, surrounded by dark, empty rooms.

My fatigue from the day's labour, the alcohol, the warm, airless atmosphere and the enchantment of holding Eloïse, the most bewitching woman in the world, gradually had its effect and, as we came alongside a chaise longue, I pulled her down onto it and started to kiss her with a passion and urgency that I hadn't known I was capable of feeling.

Of course, one thing led to another and within moments we were both on the floor and Eloïse was on top of me. She ripped my shirt open and I felt her face under my chin and then, as always, those few alarming seconds when she brushed her big white teeth against my throat. She knew it frightened me but the fact that I let her do it reassured her that I trusted her implicitly and, anyway, there is nothing like a little fear to stimulate love-making.

It would be difficult to describe to anyone the depth of my feelings for Eloïse. I recognised from the start that she was entirely capable of killing me any time she wanted but, in a strange and not fully understood way, I didn't care. Perhaps I reasoned that, as a human, my life was finite. When I must die, what better than it be by the hand of someone who loved me?

I knew it was insane but that was the way I felt about her. I even asked her once what she thought death was like – she, who was unable to die.

We spent the night together in that room, Eloïse and I, curled up in each other's arms, in front of the fire.

I never found out what she was celebrating that night or for what the elaborate scene-setting was intended. It was just a small event in my strange life with Eloïse, Countess Zaleska.

Belle's Diary

Friday, 30 June 1972

Saw that Jack guy in the Nag's last night. First time in absolute ages. In fact, I thought he'd moved away – his little cottage looks shut up tight whenever I pass it; there seems to be new people there. There were no 'FOR SALE' signs so I supposed he'd let it and meant to come back. Then last night he walked into the pub like he'd never been away.

He looked OK too. Seemed to have lost that hangdog look he used to have – like he'd got the weight of the world on his shoulders! Wasn't intending to stay long, apparently, drank his beer down like it was going out of fashion but, at the same time, he seemed totally relaxed – no longer restless and uneasy as before, when it was like he was always waiting for someone.

I'd had a few white wines and was feeling a bit relaxed so I went up to the bar and stood behind him. When my drink came, I tried the old 'damsel in distress' routine and told the barman I'd forgotten my purse – he didn't believe it of course 'cos I'd already used it to pay for the first three glasses – but this Jack guy fell for it straightaway and, like the gentleman he is, offered to pay. I let him so as to have a reason to talk to him.

Truth is, I was just a teeny bit tipsy and I may have overdone the 'come hither' chat. But he didn't seem to mind and, for the first time, he actually looked hard at me and seemed inclined to talk. Whatever had happened to him had really perked him up and soon he was smiling at me and chatting away. He seemed like a man who'd just been told he'd won the lottery and whose cares were all behind him.

But I know different! That old sixth sense of mine kicked in – the one that makes the locals say I'm a witch. If only they knew… My great grandmother had the *gift* and everyone was scared of her. Anyway, whatever… I soon picked up vibes from Jack.

There's a woman in it! The sort of woman who's different enough to pull a bloke like him. It's that French 'macho' thing – whenever they have a woman on the go, their confidence goes up in leaps and bounds. I gave him the old 'long time no see' line to see if he would tell me anything but he didn't go for it and just agreed with me.

He must be shagging someone because he didn't have that predatory '*en manque*' look that some men get when they haven't had sex for a while.

This Jack is totally at ease with his life now and that surprised me a bit, given the stress I'd seen in him before. I asked him to come and sit with me and he did and we talked about everything – books, films, different countries. It was great but it was also obvious that he was just being polite, sociable, and he had no interest in chatting me up.

I tried to steer the conversation back to him and his current situation but he skilfully dodged that and, by the time we parted, I still hadn't found out. Even asking him outright whether he had left his cottage didn't get a straight answer. He just said that he'd let it so that he could do some travelling. Further than that, he wouldn't be drawn.

We were sitting outside so that I could smoke a roll-up and, as soon as it got a bit dark, he was looking for excuses to leave. He gave me a peck on the cheek in a brotherly sort of way and was gone into the night.

My vibes seemed to have deserted me. All I got was the feeling that there was definitely a woman in his life and that he was very happy about it.

Perhaps the white wine is blocking my reception!

Chapter 8

*'Doubt… is an illness that comes from knowledge
and leads to madness.'*
Gustave Flaubert, *Memoirs of a Madman*

Next day, leaving Eloïse to her daytime rest, I plunged into my gardening work. It was so relaxing and stress-free that it was little wonder I was able to manage without any medication. Thoughts of the trauma surrounding the 'Event' were long since cast from my mind and I felt both physically and mentally fit. Any doubts I may once have entertained about living with Eloïse were also quite dispelled and my only lingering care was my previous experience that nothing good lasts forever.

My method of working was, like my life, erratic. What I now termed the 'secret garden' was, after much hard work, cleared for planting and I decided to give myself a break and do something different while I ruminated on what to plant there. In the back of my mind, I wanted to include the lake in my long-term plans for the grounds. At one time joined to the now dried-up moat, the lake too was badly overgrown. Quite large, with its own tumbledown boathouse and a small island, the lakeside was taken over by shrubs in many places. Small trees had fallen or been blown into the water, forming stagnant lagoons. Many of the shrubs were out of control and some, lacking pruning, had bolted and overhung or dipped into the water, rendering sections of bank virtually impassable. The larger trees had also become too big and cast shadows over the surface, making the whole area shaded and sombre.

I stood for a while contemplating this rather dismal scene, yet plotting in my mind the possible beauty of the place once returned to its former glory. Finally, having determined a rough outline in my mind, I made my way back to the house to collect some waders and a bush saw. There was no sign of life there and I knew Eloïse would be 'resting' during this time of bright sunshine.

Back at the lake, I picked the most obvious of the small trees collapsed into the water, sawed through the shattered trunk that held it still to its roots and tried to pull it out with the intention of dragging it back on to the bank to be cut up. To my dismay, I couldn't move it and guessed that one or more of the sunken branches must be stuck in the mud of the lake bottom. By a supreme effort, I pulled the trunk a few feet up the bank. One half-sunken branch in particular seemed to resist all my efforts to drag it clear. Carefully testing the depth of the water with my waders on, I found that I could walk along the bottom without sinking too far into the mud. By the time I reached the branch in question, the brackish, smelly water was up to my waist. The branch still resisted and I put all my strength and weight into one almighty heave. The bough moved up towards the surface but as it did so I felt a weird brushing against my legs, as if a huge fish had nosed into them.

It is not unknown for fish in old lakes to grow to a large size. The chances of a catfish, I thought, were slim but there were pike, and even carp can reach huge proportions over time. This was no fish though because it did not make off but continued to nose into my legs. Suddenly, I became afraid. The dark water prevented me from seeing far below the surface but something pale, something very big, was bumping against me. It was then that I saw a blue rope, taut and rising from the water, hooked at one end around the branch I was trying to lift. I saw it but it was too late to save myself from tipping backwards over it. I pivoted head down into the lake. Fighting to regain my footing and blind in the muddy water, I fell heavily against a soft, yielding mass bobbing just below the surface. As I came up, I slipped and fell again, this time right on top of it. Thoroughly alarmed, I waded to the bank, crawled up it and lay, gasping, as the stinking water drained off me.

When my heart had stopped thumping, I forced myself to look at the scene. The mass was close to the surface now, bobbing just a few inches below the dark water with its weed and slime, making arabesques in the currents caused by my frantic splashing. I could see that it was held there by the blue nylon rope that I had tripped over. Forcing myself into the dark, putrid water, I used my garden knife to reach under the floating object and cut the rope. Instantly, the sodden mass popped to the surface but I could still not make out what it was. Climbing out again, I caught my breath and then tried again to drag the tree trunk out. It seemed incredibly heavy for a small tree until I noticed that the other end of the blue rope was hooked on a branch and, as I was pulling the tree, the dark shape came with it.

When at last it was all up onto the bank, I couldn't face a close inspection because I desperately needed to go back to the house to change and shower and wash my hair.

Feeling much better and a bit sheepish about how easily I got spooked, I made my way back to the lake, taking some bottles of beer with me. Nothing had moved! Approaching cautiously, I prodded the shape with a pitchfork that was lying nearby. The shape appeared to be wrapped in what looked like an old, quilted coat. When I turned it over, the hood, heavy with water, fell back, revealing a swollen, bloated face!

Somewhere, someone was shouting – a raucous yet hoarse scream. It was me.

Long, dark, wet hair framed a face that, in spite of the swelling and waterlogged skin, I recognised immediately. It was Lorca.

Poor, caring, kind-hearted Lorca – my friend and support when I first came to the cottage and probably the only person at that time who had any good feelings towards me. I leapt back and for a moment the ground seemed to tilt up vertically so that I was horizontal to it and then seemed to roll over my head. I was flat out on the ground, heart racing, unable to comprehend the enormity of what was happening. Had I really just dragged the lifeless, bloated, sightless corpse of my former housekeeper and friend out of that slimy lake? I sat on the grass waiting for my mind to clear, desperate to discover that none of it was real – that I had experienced some sort of waking nightmare that would eventually dissolve and leave me sitting alone by the lake.

But it did not dissolve; the nightmare did not go away. Minutes later, when I dared to look again, Lorca's hideous, accusing eyes stared back at me and I felt in them reproach, surprise and the question 'why?' I couldn't look any more. I ran until I reached the secret garden, slumped down on a bench and cried my eyes out, huge, racking sobs that eventually relieved me and calmed me down.

What had happened? How had Lorca ended up in that overgrown stagnant lake? How could she know it even existed? Still calming down, I tried to apply some sort of logic. I have some medical knowledge – or rather forensic learning – and knew that her body could not have been long in the water or I would not have recognised her. What was she even doing here when she should have been back in Romania? Logic brought more sinister thoughts: this was no accidental drowning, unless she had tied the rope from the branch around her own waist!

I let these painful thoughts stay jumbled in my head to allow my brain to subdue the panic that had built up in me. All the questions would have to wait because I was now desperate to find something I could use to cover her up, to hide her indignity, to do the decent thing and cover her ghastly vulnerability. Stupid, I know, but we react in odd ways when faced with the illogical and in a state of shock.

Running back to the yard, I found an old canvas tarpaulin in the barn. I ran back to her and, forcing myself not to look at her face with its accusing eyes, covered her gently, making sure that every part was hidden from view. After that, I felt a little better and returned to my seat in the garden to think things through and drink as much beer as I could.

My first instinct was to go to the pub and use their telephone to alert the police but, even as I considered this, I dismissed it completely. How could we call the police? They would launch an immediate enquiry; they would make it a crime scene, a suspicious death at the very least. There would be dozens of officers, detectives and forensic personnel tramping all over us, asking questions. 'Who lives here?' 'Did you know the deceased?' 'What was she doing here?' Then of course there was Eloïse. I could never let her submit to all sorts of impertinent questions – identity checks – hers and mine. We were off the radar here. No rates, no electricity or water bills. We didn't exist, officially, and that's how we wanted it. Now we would be suspects. They would certainly do blood tests and then the truth about my beautiful Eloïse would be revealed and the resulting media frenzy would overwhelm her... 'REAL LIVE VAMPIRE DISCOVERED... ALIEN GENES... RITUAL MURDER.'

I started to sweat. The thought of it appalled me. I know all about the police and their methods – knew about them first hand. No, absolutely not! We could not tell them. It was my decision and I alone would take responsibility for it. I would hide Lorca – a burial in some nice part of the grounds – with dignity and whatever religious service I could manage.

I felt the panic rise up in me again. I couldn't understand why I felt so guilty. It wasn't as if we had killed her or, indeed, had any part in her death. I really believed she was in Romania with her family... yes, a secret burial... I wouldn't even tell Eloïse. After all, what crime would I commit? Not reporting a death? Concealing a burial? Both were criminal offences but not as serious as destroying our life together. I had to protect Eloïse. I felt responsible for her. And, anyway, I loved her so much that I would do anything for her.

Further than that, I could not think. When life becomes too awful to bear, the brain shuts down and a survival instinct takes over. Let the future implications lie dormant while you deal with the immediate threat.

Clean clothes and a shave made me feel slightly better but I was dreading my evening with Eloïse. I didn't want to tell her what had happened and yet she always seemed to know instinctively when something was troubling me. I hated to lie to her but it seemed the only response to a dreadful situation.

She was sitting in an armchair reading when I entered the parlour and she got up to kiss me, as usual. I launched into a carefully censored account of my day's activities in an attempt to divert my mind away from anything she might pick up on. She did, it's true, give me a long, quizzical look but I babbled on about my plans for the secret garden and think I actually convinced myself that all was well.

Eloïse had cooked me a wonderful meal of Hungarian

goulash, which normally I love but that evening, understandably, my appetite had deserted me. It was, though, the only food I'd had all day and I tried hard to eat as much as I could, washing it down with heavy red wine.

She was not so easily fooled. As I helped her clear away the dishes, she asked me again if anything was troubling me. That gave me a chance to make some excuse about being out in the sun too long and feeling a bit dehydrated, adding quickly that I really fancied a pint and did she mind if I popped out to the pub for an hour. She agreed, as I knew she would. Eloïse never drank alcohol but she seemed to understand my need for it. Peter, it seemed, had liked a drink.

A quick kiss, a promise not to be late and I was out of the house and along the lane with the intention of drowning my sorrows – an unfortunate habit that had cost me dear in the past.

A couple of times, I stopped and listened, thinking I'd heard light footfalls behind me. I could not be sure. To my continuing horror, I could not shake the vision of poor Lorca's cold body lying under that old tarpaulin. Shuddering, I moved on again quickly, longing to see the welcoming lights of the pub. Images of Lorca's swollen and flaking white face swept into my mind and, for the first time since I moved in with Eloïse, I experienced that old fear that made my back feel stone cold and yet brought beads of sweat to my forehead. The noises increased and I imagined a slithery, wet sound just behind me that ceased when I stopped and started again as I moved off.

Imagination can be a remorseless enemy and, in my mind's eye, I imagined Lorca, grey, amorphous and slimy, reaching out to touch my back. At one point, the sensation became so tangible that I actually broke into a run and did not slow down even when the lights of the pub came into view.

Out of breath when I reached the door, I stopped and

forced myself to be calm before going in, composing my features to what I felt would be a normal, casual look. Once inside, everything changed. The cheerful lighting, the burble of conversation, the smiles from the barmaid, Frankie; it was as if I had passed into another world.

Ordering a pint, I looked around to see if there was anyone I knew to talk to and, by so doing, keep my demons at bay. Over in the corner by the chimney, her usual place, was Belle. She'd seen me and looked across as if expecting me to join her. That could be a mixed blessing because, though I enjoyed her company, she seemed always to be probing me, fishing for information and then giving me knowing looks and the occasional sly wink, as if we were complicit in some sort of private knowledge that others could not share. Normally, I would not have minded; she could be charming and witty and good company but tonight there was something in her look that seemed to say, 'I know what you've done…'

So when Mark walked over and put his pint down next to mine, I saw an opportunity to keep away from her.

Mark was a big guy and yet he had an office job not requiring his sort of physique. He also seemed to think that intellectually he was way ahead of most of the locals and was probably right. He conveyed the idea that he and I were automatically linked by some sort of superiority of intellect and that there was a certain amount of mutual kudos to be gained by our talking together. As it happened, I was pleased to have someone to talk to about anything that would take my thoughts away from that huge cloud of darkness that Lorca's death had lodged in my mind, lurking there to strike at me as soon as a void opened in my brain.

To tell the truth, I can't remember anything we talked about except that Mark's face was earnest and serious and that I must have mumbled some apposite replies because he continued for a long while. As soon as he was distracted, I excused myself, hurried towards the toilets and, when he wasn't looking veered towards the back exit and the beer garden, to make good my escape, only to bump into Belle who was preparing a roll-up that I suspected, and smelled, contained more than a pinch of cannabis.

'Hi Jack!'

She stood up from her table and neatly intercepted me.

'Long time no see. I heard you'd left the cottage. Where're you living now then?'

I had to admire her cheek. Subtlety was not Belle's way but she seemed to be able to disguise her nosiness as concern for my welfare. Although I'd intended to leave, I hadn't had enough beer to dull the pain of Lorca's death. With some misgivings, I offered to buy Belle a drink and bought another pint for myself. Back outside with the drinks, I decided to put up with her smoking and sat down opposite. She thanked me as I handed her a huge glass of white wine with ice, took a deep drag on her roll-up and closed her eyes for a moment as she exhaled. She looked straight at me in such a way that I knew she was trying to probe my mind. I'd had that feeling before with her but that night it was very obvious.

'So where did you say you were living now, Jack?' We'd been through all that the last time we met.

'I didn't.' I tried not to sound rude but her nosiness was beginning to annoy me. It sounded a bit abrupt, so I softened it.

'Well, you know, Belle, travelling to Paris and then back here for a few days staying with friends. Needed to check on the cottage.'

She didn't believe me, I could see that from her grin, but she was astute enough not to push it. Things went a bit quiet after that and I cast around in my mind for something to say to change the subject.

Every time I was left to my own thoughts, I had a flashback

of poor Lorca's grey face, the stagnant water draining from her hair. I shuddered and Belle saw it. For a split second, a look of horror crossed her face as though she had seen the same nightmare picture. But I knew that could not be the case. Picking up my pint, I glanced around me, emptied it and got up to get another.

When I came back, Belle was smoking again. She looked up and asked, 'Want to talk?'

What did she know, this girl? How could she know anything?

'I'm sorry, Belle. I'm poor company tonight, I know. It's just tiredness. The trip from Paris was delayed… I didn't sleep well… and today I stayed too long in the sun.'

She smiled, 'I don't believe a word of it,' but she didn't actually say that.

I was feeling increasingly paranoid, hemmed in, as if everyone was watching and scrutinising me. I needed to leave. I had this stupid feeling that they were all staring at me. I put the rest of my beer down in three gulps and forced a smile at Belle.

'Please excuse me. I need to get my head down… been out in the sun too much.'

I wondered whether I had already said that. I couldn't remember. I was coming apart and I couldn't stop it. I needed to get out. My heart sank when she replied,

'I'll walk with you, Jack.'

Rising hastily, she picked up her handbag.

It was the last thing I wanted and I stretched out my hand, palm facing her.

'No, really Belle, it's OK.'

She was adamant though; I could see it in her face.

'Oh, Jack, a gentleman like you… refusing to walk a poor girl home in the dark!'

I knew I was beaten, trapped, so I agreed at once, saying clumsily that I didn't want her to leave just because I had to go. She laughed, gave me her arm and started for the door.

My brain was racing overtime; I couldn't turn off down to the manor or she would know immediately that I was staying there. I'd have to walk past and continue with her as far as the crossroads where she lived, in the cottage next to the butcher's shop.

We were both a bit tipsy and I'm not sure who was walking who because we both stumbled at least once.

Outside her door, she invited me in but I made the same excuse, saying that I was tired and a bit drunk – which wasn't actually far from the truth. Fortunately, she didn't insist and, after a quick peck on the cheek, went in and shut the door. Relieved, I turned back up towards the pub and the lane to the manor. But as I did so, I realised that I must pass the darkened bus shelter where Eloïse, in her various guises, had first ambushed me. As I came alongside the shelter, a feeling of uneasiness swept over me. The interior, as usual, was pitch black and yet I could not resist staring into it. Suddenly, I caught a whiff of that sweet, musky scent that I knew so well. My heart thumped and I stopped in mid-stride.

'Eloïse?' I called out timidly. There was no answer and, relieved, I went to move on. Suddenly, she was at my side with a speed that startled me even though I was used to it.

'So, Jacques,' she whispered in French, 'this is your little girlie from the pub that kept you from me this night?'

I tried to decide whether there was sarcasm or anger in her tone but, as usual, her words told me nothing about her feelings.

'Little girlie?' I forced a laugh. 'No, that was Belle, Eloïse, the local witch.'

I tried to keep my tone light and a bit jokey but my heart

was still thumping from the sudden surprise of meeting her here. She took my hand. Her bony grip felt cool compared with Belle's fleshy and warm clasp. Stupidly, I felt guilty about being caught with Belle although I had done nothing to reproach myself for by simply walking her home. Any man, I reasoned, gentleman that is, would have felt obligated.

I was glad of these thoughts because I was still not sure to what extent Eloïse could read my mind or whether it was just astute observation on her part. Boldly, I decided that attack was the best defence.

'So, what are *you* doing here, Eloïse? Spying on me?'

Of course, it fell short of the desired effect.

'Need I spy on you, Jacques?'

I couldn't see her face in the darkness so I had no idea from her neutral tone whether she was angry with me. I felt, still, that I had to defend myself.

'Eloïse, you must understand that I have found everything I want in my life in knowing you and I would never jeopardise that.'

Clumsy and fulsome it might have sounded, but it seemed to have impressed her because she squeezed my hand and suddenly her mouth was on mine and, despite my tiredness, despite the alcohol and despite my heartbreak about Lorca, I felt my body and soul respond to her.

I don't remember much about the walk back. I know Eloïse chatted gaily and kept stopping to kiss and embrace me. Then, we were in bed and all my black thoughts were banished as we merged our existence and sank, eventually, into a dark, comfortable nothingness.

Next morning, I awoke as usual to find the bed empty and my mind instantly full of black thoughts and despair. All the tragedy of Lorca's death swept back in, compared with which my hangover was the merest thing. I knew that if I just lay there, the despair and mental blackness would overwhelm me and so, risking the headache, which would normally have kept me there, I slid out of bed and staggered to the bathroom. As the thoughts of Lorca flooded back, I felt violently sick but could not vomit.

A hurried cup of black coffee and I was out into the garden with a half-formed plan to bury Lorca's body somewhere nice, trying to hide the whole terrible business. Dragging a spade behind me, I went straight to the secret garden and made for the dew-soaked tarpaulin I'd used the day before.

Steeling myself for the gruesome sight, I lifted the material hesitantly; the underside was crawling with slugs but then, to my great terror, I saw – nothing. Her body was gone. Stupidly, I looked around me, as if a corpse could have moved itself! Nothing. No trace, not even an indentation in the grass. How could she be gone? Had some wild animal dragged her away? And if so, what kind of animal would that be to drag away a fully grown woman and then come back and replace the cover?

I ran to the house, grabbed a bottle of Peter's best red wine, uncorked it and took a huge gulp, then took it with me back to the garden. It was the only strong drink we had. I made a mental note to buy some brandy.

Sitting on the bench, I stared at the empty tarpaulin; then, as the dew soaked through the seat of my jeans, it put a thought in my mind. Going back to the cover, I searched around it for any traces left in the dew on the grass. Sure enough, looking closely, I was able to discern slight marks resembling those of a cat's paw prints, except much bigger. There were no drag marks so the body must have been lifted clear of the grass and carried. Instantly, I thought of the footmarks in my cottage on the tiles in the kitchen – after the cat had been killed. Lorca thought they were human and asked me why I had a woman in the house.

Sickness rose in my stomach as the clues I should have seen before assembled in my dull brain. I hadn't told anyone about finding Lorca, not even Eloïse; especially not Eloïse. So who else could have known the body was there? Only two people had access to the grounds of the manor and, if I hadn't moved her, it must have been Eloïse. The marks on the grass matched those in the cottage and I always suspected that she may have been inside before I invited her. I knew only too well how strong she was. She could easily have carried a body over her shoulder.

Hardly daring to follow this train of thought, I bent down and followed the faint tracks. Those leading away from the cover were deeper than those leading to it, suggesting that a heavy weight was being carried. I followed them carefully through the garden and out into a small patch where I was growing sunflowers and was just able to discern a track between the tall stalks. There, right in the centre of the flowers was an oblong of recently disturbed soil about the size of a grave.

Back in the house, I slumped on the sofa and opened another bottle of wine. Drink as I would, I couldn't dull the pain of my thoughts. There were too many questions I could not answer. Had Eloïse found Lorca's body, by chance, on her night prowls around the garden? Was that before she ambushed me at the bus shelter or later, in the early hours, when I was asleep? How could she know that I would pass that shelter, with Belle, unless she followed us from the pub? Did she have any involvement in Lorca's death?

To this last question, frightening answers were suggesting themselves. I remembered how Lorca's neck rolled as though it was broken. Eloïse, I knew, was capable of snapping a human spine; I was sure of it. But why would she? She didn't know Lorca except by name from the times I had referred to her as my housekeeper. I could not believe that of her. If I had had the slightest doubt about Eloïse, I would never have moved in with her.

And yet... and yet... something was niggling away at me. My greatest fear, that something external beyond my control might change my happiness with Eloïse, was entirely misplaced; the danger, I now realised, was from within my mind, my thoughts, my suspicions, the tiny but pervasive doubts, starting to undermine the trust I had in her.

It seemed obvious that the police, if we'd called them, would have only two suspects: me and Eloïse. And as I knew it could not be me... I dismissed that train of thought and swore to myself there and then that I would never consider Eloïse as a suspect; to do so would go against everything I had come to know of her.

So, I reasoned, there must be a third party. Lorca did not snap her own neck, tie a rope around her waist, fasten it to a fallen tree and then jump in the lake! Nor did she get up from under a tarpaulin, dig her own grave and then, somehow, fill it in. I didn't have to be Sherlock Holmes to work that out. So that meant we were both in danger. Eloïse, I knew, could look after herself. I had witnessed her speed and strength, her enhanced hearing and sense of smell, her ability to see in the dark. I was by far the weaker one and, though fit and strong, would be vulnerable to an attacker hidden in the jungle that was a good part of the grounds.

From that moment, I resolved to carry the old, bolt-action shotgun with me whenever I was in the gardens. It was single shot and of small 4.10 calibre but it could really hurt a man at close range.

Back in the secret garden, with the gun propped against a nearby tree, I tried to lose my thoughts by concentrating on the job in hand and surprising Eloïse with a beautiful hidden garden. Even so, I found myself looking up frequently, scanning the hedges and shrubs.

That evening, Eloïse was waiting for me when I came in from the garden. She was resplendent in a long, Edwardian dress, her hair swept up in a sort of bun with ringlets around it. She was wearing her jewellery and, if I had not known otherwise, I would have thought we were invited for dinner at a palace. She came close to me and touched my face affectionately and I noticed her fingers, normally so cool, were warm as though she had been holding them to one of the oil lamps. Something really fragrant was cooking, the wind-up gramophone was playing and the champagne she handed me was cold and sparkling.

I could not hold back a sigh of happiness. It was as though all the troubles of the last two days had disappeared and we were back to our normal happy routine, my fears pushed so far to the back of my mind that I wondered whether it had all been a nightmare and I had dreamed the whole thing: sunstroke or something. I resolved never to go back to that patch of garden in case Lorca's grave *was* there, which meant I couldn't go on believing it hadn't happened. A kiss from Eloïse brought me back from these macabre thoughts. She gave me a clean shirt and a dark suit and ushered me off to the bath she had filled for me.

The food was excellent, as usual, something Hungarian she said and, of course, there was wine for me and candlelight and music. Eloïse was even more attentive than usual to my every comfort. Most people fall in love only a few times in their life but I fell in love with Eloïse every night – though that night I felt a bit guilty at having suspected she could ever do anything bad. Predictably, the evening ended in love-making.

But during sex, a curious and unsettling thing happened. We were in Eloïse's bedroom in the derelict part of the house, the room very dimly lit by starlight through the single, curtainless, cobwebbed window. She was straddling me on the bed and I could just make out the silhouette of her upper body, seeming to tower over my prostrate form. The musty air was heavy and still with that closeness that usually precedes a storm. Indeed, a few flickerings at the window confirmed that lightning was about, though oddly there had been no rumblings of thunder. Behind the low, almost growling sounds that Eloïse always made during our love-making, I could just hear the first swish of rain.

Suddenly, lightning lit up the sky and the room and in that split second of intense light, I saw Eloïse – but not the beautiful woman I was so in love with! I saw the silhouette of a form I can only liken to an Egyptian God; a profile that looked like a thin, angular trunk surmounted by a jackal-like head but seen only in profile, a bit like the figures painted on the walls of Egyptian tombs; human-like bodies with the head of a dog or bird mounted sideways. It was a split-second silhouette that made me cry out and shudder.

It was too stupid of me! I could only hope that Eloïse thought it was a positive reaction to our climaxing together. She paused for a second and then carried on until she too gasped and made a low, moaning sound, unique to her and produced only when our love-making was a special success.

My eyes were wide open then, waiting to see if the lightning would strike again. Eloïse was no longer sitting upright. I could feel her lying on top of me, her face at my neck. And then I felt those big teeth nibbling gently along my throat. But this time, I was unable to stop the fear and revulsion rising in me and my whole body tensed for just a few seconds. I knew instinctively that she had felt it too. She rolled off me onto her side of the bed and I could feel her eyes on me. I knew she could see in the dark so I forced myself to smile – whether it looked convincing or not, I had no way of knowing.

'Jacques?' she said in her husky voice. '*Qu'est ce qu'il ya?* (What's the matter?)' Before I could think of a reply, she continued in English. 'I thought we had put all that behind us, yet you seem still afraid of me. Did you really think I would bite you just now? Tell me what's wrong. You've been jumpy and behaving oddly recently. That's why I followed you to the pub the other night. It wasn't to spy on you, I promise. But even there, you could not relax. Now, tell me, or do you want me to read your mind?' She laughed to break the tension.

While she was talking, it gave me the chance to think of an excuse, a feasible explanation. I put my arms around her and pulled her to me so that I could kiss her in an attempt to reassure her.

'*Tu m'excuse, trés aimée* (I'm sorry, my love).' I told her that I'd been having nightmares again. I dare not lie to her because I was not sure to what extent she could read my mind. I'd already told her a bit about my past and how a reoccurring nightmare plagued me, so there was an element of truth in my excuse. I'd never told her about the 'Event' though.

There was a long silence and I was beginning to think she'd seen through my avoidance tactics, when at last she said, '*Mon pauvre Jacques. T'en fais pas. Eloïse va te soigner.* (Poor Jack. Don't worry. Eloïse will look after you.)'

She giggled and snuggled up to me in a way that suggested she wanted me to make love to her over again.

I said, 'Hey, hey, I'm only human!'

And we both laughed. Putting her arms around me, she pulled me to her as if protecting a child and the last thing I remembered before falling asleep was the beautiful musky scent of her body.

BELLE'S DIARY

Wednesday, 20 September 1972

Feeling upbeat today! Don't know why, particularly. No hangover even though I tied one on a bit at the pub with that guy Jack. Don't know why I always say, 'that guy', instead of just 'Jack'. I suppose it's because no matter how often we talk, he still seems a bit insular. Talk about erecting a barrier! There's definitely something about him. I can't say *weird* because he seems such a nice bloke but he's got so much baggage, mentally I mean. Sometimes he appears almost depressed but then he laughs or tells a joke and it seems to disappear.

It's his eyes. My nan was more of a witch than I will ever be and she would always say, 'The eyes have it. They are the windows of the soul.' People don't go for that these days. Nobody believes in *souls* any more – how stupid is that? His eyes are empty.

Last night, he was in a bad place, this Jack. Tried to hide it but no chance with me. He was physically shaking at one point. And talk about drink! He must have had at least five pints of Guinness while he was with me. But it didn't kill his demons.

Walking back, he kept looking over his shoulder, even though it was pitch dark and when we got to the bus shelter, he tried to get me to cross the road. Perhaps he was afraid I might pull him into it and rape him!

Wouldn't come into the house when I asked him. I thought

I'd made it pretty obvious that… well, he could've come in and stayed. Instead, he gives me this brotherly peck on the cheek and he's gone.

Perhaps it's just as well. I can't fight his demons as well as my own. Don't know where he went though. Back up towards the pub, not towards his cottage and, anyway, that's rented out now.

Much as I like a bit of company, I'm wary of him. My sorcery tells me he's dangerous.

CHAPTER 9

'I became insane, with long intervals of horrible sanity'
EDGAR ALLAN POE

I woke to an empty bed and with a bit of a hangover. The morning was grey and sunless. Even the garden could not lift my spirits.

At first, I threw all my efforts into the secret garden project but my mind kept coming back to that unmarked grave in the sunflower patch and poor, dead Lorca under the cold clay. I would not let myself go near it but time and again found myself looking towards it as if expecting to see some ghastly apparition walk out between the huge stems of sunflowers.

Without bright sunlight, the garden was dull and formless. That day, nothing moved in it, not a bird, a butterfly nor even a rabbit or squirrel. I could not remember it being such a mournful place before. In spite of my best efforts at distraction, I found myself thinking about the situation again and again. It seemed obvious that Lorca had met a silent death – that she had been murdered, but why and by whom? And why here? Although I tried everything to shut out the thought, Eloïse kept creeping back into my mind. There were, after all, only two of us here. Who else would have access? The lake was hidden, overgrown, probably unknown to anyone but us. We were always here so, when and how could such a terrible crime have been committed without us knowing about it? What great strength would it take to break someone's neck? And who did I know who could do such a thing? And who buried her?

No one will ever know how hard I tried to steer my thoughts – indeed, my suspicions – away from Eloïse. But it all just kept coming back to her. I looked at the shotgun (I carried it everywhere now) and for a second I thought of blowing my brains out. I loved Eloïse so much that I could not live if it meant a lifetime of suspicion undermining my feelings for her. All I wanted was to get back to where we were before. It was as if the 'Event' was happening all over again.

I opened the bolt on the rifle and flicked out the cartridge. I was being stupid. I loved her and I would continue to do so and I wouldn't let anything change that.

What possible motive could Eloïse have for harming Lorca? She wasn't a jealous person and anyway there was nothing for her to be jealous about. I had not seen nor heard from Lorca for nearly a year and had no reason to believe I would ever see her again.

I carried on frantically cutting at the undergrowth and tried to dismiss the whole, sad business from my troubled mind.

Towards late afternoon, I was feeling easier, having managed to a certain extent to stave off all those black thoughts by forcing my mind to concentrate on what I was doing and meticulously planning the design in my mind, to a point where I'd earmarked suitable shrubs for certain places. Even the sun came out to reinforce my change of mood.

Something suddenly made me look up and I fancied I saw a fleeting movement among the dense bushes to my left. Staring at the spot, it seemed to me that the leaves were moving in the wrong direction – counter to the breeze, which invariably sprang up at that time of day. Simultaneously the sunlight that had begun to filter down through the leaves overhead dimmed as a dark cloud passed before the sun. Foliage that had been bright green moments before became dark, almost black. Wood pigeons flew up suddenly, the loud beating of their wings startling me. Everything went very quiet, an oppressive unnatural silence that seemed to descend on me. Adrenalin from some primitive fight-or-flight reflex flooded my brain without giving it an explanation.

At some point, I must have picked up the shotgun because I found myself working the bolt and scanning the shrubbery at the same time. There was no conscious plan; I just followed my instinct and stepped into the tall rhododendrons to my left. I didn't know whether I was hiding or hunting, I just crouched there holding the gun ready, mind blank, following the instinctive reactions of my body.

It was so quiet. An absolute and unnatural silence descended on the place. There was no sound, no movement, just as if I were standing in a giant black and white photograph of a garden. It seemed even darker, with black clouds filling the sky but instead of the fresh smell of impending rain, a stifling, airless, foetid smell filled the air, tainted with the stench of stagnant water.

Once again, I found myself staring in the direction of the sunflower patch. Above the shrubs, I could just make out the heads of the giant flowers on their six-foot stalks. Oddly, in spite of the complete stillness of the air, the flower heads were moving, tilting as it were, a few at a time, advancing in my direction and that slow progression towards me added to my fervid imaginings of what was causing it, pushing me into panic. I fled in the direction of the house, not daring to look back.

Even in the house, I did not recover my composure. Eloïse did not seem to be up and about and the rooms seemed cold and empty. It was too early to light the lamps and the gloom added to my depression.

I wanted to go back, to return to that wonderful, happy time before I had found Lorca's body but I couldn't get back, any more than I could go back to before the 'Event'. Then I reasoned that I *had* surmounted that, eventually, and I could get through this. With Eloïse's help.

I had an overwhelming urge to confide in her, tell her the whole story. She would know what to do; she had the wisdom of several lifetimes behind her. But something made me hesitate. There had been various opportunities to tell her the tragic news, yet I could not understand why I had shunned doing so. Some half-formed thought fluttering in the back of my mind held me back. Suspicion? Guilt? I needed to understand what it was. I had been wrong about so many things in my life and had no confidence in my decision-making anymore and so, logically, I felt I needed to seek advice, and who better to give it than the person I loved and trusted?

I determined to tell her everything after our evening meal and to act on her advice. Just making that decision brought me relief.

Eloïse, apparently, had no surprises in store for me that evening and dinner passed uneventfully. She seemed a bit quiet, subdued even, but not enough to give me cause for concern. I drank more red wine than usual to give myself a bit of courage and, as soon as the table was cleared and she was sitting next to me on the sofa, I launched into my carefully prepared story.

'Eloïse, you remember my housekeeper back at the cottage, Lorca?'

'The Romanian? You told me about her.'

'Yes. Her name was really Relorca, or something like that.'

Eloïse looked straight at me and said slowly, 'She's dead.'

I just stared at her, too astonished to speak. Finally, I managed a weak, 'How did you know that?'

'Oh really, Jacques! Sometimes you can be remarkably obtuse. I found her body in the grounds, where you had covered her with a cloth.'

'And… and…?' I asked incredulously.

'And I buried her. You must have realised that she didn't just walk off!' For once, irritation sounded in her voice.

'But why did you not tell me?'

'Why did you not tell me you had found her, Jack?' she countered.

Eloïse didn't appear the slightest bit perturbed, as if finding a dead body in your garden was an everyday occurrence.

There followed a long silence as I tried to think what to say next.

'Well, what about her?' she prompted.

I couldn't believe how casually she took this horrendous news or understand why she didn't ask me where and how I found the body.

'She was in the lake,' I blurted out at last.

'I know,' she said quietly. 'I put her there! It seemed as good a place as any.'

'*You* put her there?' I was shouting then. 'In God's name, Eloïse, why?'

'Because I killed her.'

I couldn't speak. I just stared at her, unable even to form a thought.

'*Allons, Jacques, pourquoi cette gueule?* (Come on, Jack, why the long face?)'

She leaned close to me, her heavy, black eyebrows raised and showing her lovely white teeth in a broad smile.

I suppose that, somewhere deep in my brain, I'd known

the truth all along but I wouldn't let myself go there. Against all the odds, I'd managed to convince myself otherwise. Now, my mind just could not cope with the truth. Eloïse, my perfect woman, the love of my life, my entire reason to carry on living, was telling me casually, almost flippantly, that she had killed the only other woman who had tried, in her way, to care for me since the 'Event'. Stunned, I stared dumbly at Eloïse, hoping perhaps that the whole thing was a very bad 'trip', a relapse into my earlier mental state – an hallucination from which I would soon awake, as I did eventually, after the 'Event'.

Ignoring my shocked silence, Eloïse put her arms around my neck and started to kiss me, her long, dark hair falling across my face. Incredibly, in spite of everything, I felt myself begin to respond. Her musky scent was like some sort of calming opiate and yet, at the same time, erotic and sensuous. In spite of my shock, she started to arouse me. No matter how often she did it to me, it always worked. Soon, her tall, slim body was all over me. I was long since accustomed to the coolness of her skin and her long fingers caressing me. Even the fact that those same hands had snapped Lorca's slim neck could not stop my body reacting to her. We were soon on the floor and, for a few blissful minutes, I was able to forget the horror of what she had admitted to me only moments before.

When I recovered from our frantic love-making, I didn't know what to say to Eloïse. She lay in my arms, her head on my chest. The silence grew oppressive and eventually I plucked up the courage to ask her why she had killed Lorca. She sat up and looked at me in a way that made me feel that I was stupid to ask and then, patiently, as if explaining something to a child, she whispered: 'I had to, Jacques. For us. For what we have here. What we share.'

I knew better than to interrupt.

'She came here. Looking for you, of course. I don't know how she found out about this place or what she knew about us. She came late at night, while you were sleeping. At first, she crept around outside, looking through the windows she could reach with a torch. I watched her, hoping she would go away, but then she found the front door unlocked. Hanging inside on the stair post was your coat and I could tell by the way she shone the torch over it that she recognised it. As she turned to leave, she caught me in the beam of her torch and immediately started screaming, '*Strigoi, strigoi!*' – terrible piercing screams. I had to stop her, Jacques. She was hysterical. I know these people. They come from a part of Eastern Europe that is steeped in superstition. They have hunted my people and tried to kill us for hundreds of years with their nonsense of vampires and blood sucking. They are a backward and ignorant people. She would have destroyed everything we have here. Eventually, someone would have believed her and come here looking, searching, intent on exposing us. I could not let that happen, Jacques. You must understand that. Tell me you do…?'

Her great, black eyes bore into mine, looking inside my head, no doubt, trusting what she could see there rather than any words I was about to say. I opened my mouth to reply and then closed it again. I had no response for her. I understood the logic of what she said, the paramount need to protect us. It was instinctive to her and, as she saw it, perfectly justified. But killing a human being? Not some anonymous enemy but a warm, loving person – a friend who was probably just trying to look after me. I felt sick to my stomach at the thought of it. Eloïse was watching me closely, reading my mind perhaps, and calculating her next move.

'Now you hate me,' she whispered at last. 'You have always feared me. Now you hate me too. Oh Jacques, what will become of us now?'

I had no answer to give and just looked at her as she continued.

'Don't you see, Jacques? If you let this come between us, your friend will have died in vain. Tell me honestly what would you have done?'

I'd been thinking the same thing.

'Tried to reason with her…' I blurted out. 'Tried to reassure her that I was OK and that she should accept that, grateful as I was, I didn't need her help anymore and that she should leave me alone – go away and forget everything… begged her even.'

'Oh come on, Jacques, do you think that someone concerned about you enough to come creeping about this place on her own, in the middle of the night, would just forget everything because you asked her nicely? She would have told someone and where would we have been then? Just sitting here waiting for the knock at the door and our life together lost?'

'We could still get that knock…' I broke in. 'Do you think for one moment, Eloïse, that she won't be missed… eventually? Suppose she told someone where she was going?'

Eloïse continued to watch me closely. She reached up and took my face in her long, cool hands, as a mother would caress a child. She kissed me.

'*Calme-toi, Jacques.* Just calm down. No more bad things are going to happen. She was the only chink in your armour. No one else will be looking for you, for us. Listen to me. I have had a hundred years of looking out for myself, against all sorts of people in many different countries. Believe me, I know what to do. The only problem, the only thing we have to fear, is your human conscience. *You* are the only risk now, to both of us. Just concentrate on coming to terms with what has happened and leave everything else to me. Do you promise me, Jack?'

I nodded. What else could I do? Deep down, I was aware that I was a loser in life – a drifter, directionless and without ambition or even a plan, who needed someone strong to cling to. Without Eloïse in my life, I had nothing, was nothing and would ever be nothing and no one.

'OK,' she said, rising. 'We will not speak of this again. I will watch you carefully to be sure you are all right and we will carry on as before. Look at me, Jacques! Say, "Yes, Eloïse".'

'Yes, Eloïse.'

'Good. Now what shall we do tomorrow night? A masked ball perhaps? Come on, tell me what you would like.'

'Surprise me,' I managed, feigning enthusiasm to please her.

'Just one last thing, Jacques. If you go to the pub, don't drink too much. It loosens your tongue. We wouldn't want to take any more risks, would we?'

I was glad that things were out in the open between us and that I no longer had to pretend in front of Eloïse. I knew I could never keep things hidden from her for long anyway. What she had said did make sense and I was pleased that she didn't go into detail about the actual killing. I couldn't let myself think about that. All I should do now was to carry on as 'normal' and hope that, with time and by trying to keep busy, things would settle down and become easier to accept. There really was no other choice.

So now there were two areas of the grounds for me to avoid – the stagnant lake and the sunflower patch. To help me keep my thoughts diverted, I brought up a dozen bottles of red wine from the cellars and kept one on the go throughout the day. I dared not go to the pub for fear of getting drunk and saying something that could cause suspicion and of coming under scrutiny of the 'Belle Witch'.

At first I believed that things were continuing as before, that the dreadful events of the past couple of weeks were receding, slowly but surely, from my mind and that we would gradually be able to delete them from our life altogether.

But something had changed. Initially, I thought it was me. I was, after all, mentally the weakest link. Eloïse would notice such things even if I'd convinced myself that my behaviour seemed normal. And then, gradually, I realised that the changes were in Eloïse. There was something different in her demeanour, something so tenuous that it took me days to perceive it and, even then, I thought it was my imagination, so infinitely subtle were the signs.

It started several nights after Eloïse made her admission to me. We'd spent a lovely evening together, quite like the old days, and I happened to mention that I missed going to the pub. When it was time for bed (at least for me) and I'd told Eloïse how tired I felt (my way of intimating that I needed a break from our frantic sex life), Eloïse kissed me goodnight in the usual way before leaving my bedroom to do whatever she did at night; I knew that she liked to prowl about in the grounds around the manor and then come back to read in the library in the derelict part of the house, or make clothes on her ancient sewing machine, bathe, wash her hair or any of the multitude of things that people do in the daytime. That she was up at night and wandering about made me feel secure in the rambling, dark, old house, knowing how capable she was at protecting us both.

This particular night, however, I was restless and slept fitfully. There was a full moon and a shaft of cold, silver light flooded my bedroom from the window where the curtain rod had collapsed, leaving the thick and dusty velvet curtain heaped on the floorboards below it. Only half awake, I was staring at this light when I thought I saw a shadow flicker across the moon beams. Following the direction of this movement, I fancied that I could just discern a dark figure, a tall silhouette that, for some reason, reminded me as before of the profile paintings you see of Anubis on the walls of Egyptian tombs.

At first, it intrigued me and I focused on it, trying to locate what innocent item in my bedroom could possibly cast such a shadow. The more I concentrated on it, the weirder it appeared. Becoming slightly alarmed, I felt that it was looking at me. I jerked upright, rocking the bed, and as I did so distinctly saw the silhouette move quickly away and was able to catch the soft closing of my bedroom door.

It quite unnerved me but I finally came to the conclusion that it had been Eloïse watching over me and it was merely a trick of the moonlight that made her shadow appear so odd.

Next afternoon, when I came in from the garden, I asked her about it. To my surprise, she denied being anywhere near my room that night.

Work in the secret garden was progressing well and proving very therapeutic for me. Only the constant feeling of being watched troubled me – that and the occasional smell of stagnant water.

My nights passed peacefully, thanks to my physical exertions in the gardens and the considerable amount of red wine that I now consumed each day. I could not, however, shake off the uneasy feeling that my relationship with Eloïse had changed. She was as wonderful with me as she had always been but again I felt, or rather sensed, a very subtle shift – so subtle that I questioned myself constantly to try to elicit what the change was but I could not, at least not at first. As before, it took the form of an almost imperceptible shift in her attitude towards me – so slight that I was able to perceive it only after a period of several weeks. Even then, it was difficult to define.

It seemed that Eloïse was observing me, watching me secretly. Several times I awoke in the night with the feeling that someone had been in my room watching me while I slept. I couldn't be sure about it but it was the same feeling as in the garden. There, it was the movement of a bush, a slight rustling of leaves, a fleeting shadow perhaps or, once, that musky scent carried on a sudden breeze.

All these things, over time, convinced me that Eloïse was watching in a way she never did before. Though I never actually saw her in the garden and I would not have confronted her even if I had. I could not bring myself to question her about it and felt certain that she no longer trusted me to keep our 'secret'. Perhaps it was not that she thought I would deliberately betray her; she knew how much I loved her and how desperate I was that our life together should continue. It seemed more as if she believed that I was weak and drank too much and would end up saying something compromising to someone in the pub. Her long life had been a chain of continuity, of survival, and I was now the weak link. I was putting her in danger.

I felt that I was then in a very difficult place. It was not that I was no longer madly in love with her; she still entranced me and aroused me every time I looked at her. It was just that my old depression had returned, as it had been before the 'Event', and I could not shake it off. Nor did I have any medication to dull it. The wine and beer helped but at a price; I was, if not exactly blind drunk, pretty much intoxicated most of the time. I felt bad about that as well. It broke my heart to be like that when Eloïse was trying so hard to help me. Usually so intelligent in all matters, she had no experience of depressive illness with its mood swings that were so alien to her and I was at great pains to hide it from her.

The logical thing for her to do would be to get rid of me. No one knew about her and, even if they did, they could never link her to Lorca and her murder, except through me. I knew that she hadn't survived all this time by not being able to take difficult decisions and I also understood, from the first, that her mindset was what we 'ordinary' humans would define as psychopathic.

My own experiences had taught me that psychopaths always get a bad press. No one seems to consider that the condition should be defined by degree. Because it can delete moral conscience from the mind, it can make what some people – indeed most people – would consider amoral or even criminal behaviour much easier and it is true that many dangerous criminals, especially so-called serial killers, have been diagnosed as psychopaths. But it does not follow that *all* psychopaths are serial killers.

Eloïse once told me that the feelings most of us call nostalgia were totally alien to her. Even her marriage and long life with Peter did not cause her any sadness when it terminated in his death. She had enjoyed being with him but felt no difference when he was no longer there, no sense of loss or sad memories of their good times together – nothing but a sense of continuity, of her own survival. She had no feelings for the past nor hopes for the future. She never felt sad or wept or had any sense of attachment to anything or anyone. Even the manor house meant nothing to her except as a small part of her present existence. The fact that it was gradually falling down around us did not concern her in the least. She had, she told me once, discovered very early in her life that she behaved and felt very differently from those around her and adopted what she described as her 'mask'. She learned how other people behaved in certain situations and imitated that behaviour and so passed as being the same. In reality, she felt none of those emotions but acting the part gave her a feeling of genuine pleasure knowing that she could so easily fool those around her. Now, the 'mask' was second nature to her and she rarely took it off in front of me. She could mimic convincingly normal reactions for any given occasion. She could read anyone like a book but was careful not to show it. After living with her for more than a year, I was well aware that she was quite 'different' and that any doubts I may have had about her story of being a hybrid soon evaporated.

Surprisingly, at the beginning, I had not felt afraid of her – though I was aware of her physical strength. Her odd habit of gently nibbling my throat with those huge white teeth had, it is true, unnerved me a bit at first but I had long since accepted it as a sign of affection, as you would let a pet dog gently bite your hand in a game. Any initial doubts I may have had about moving in with her were soon overwhelmed by a deep, aching love for her.

Now it was different, the seeds of doubt had been sown and, fight against it as I did with all my strength, the virus of suspicion was spreading through me. The logical thing to do would be to confront Eloïse about my growing concern but some sixth sense held me back.

Admitting that I doubted her would show me as dangerously weak and profoundly change the nature of our relationship. If she thought that I was becoming afraid of her, she would conclude that I was thinking of leaving and though that would mean nothing to her emotionally, it would certainly heighten her instinct of self-preservation. She would believe that, once away from her, out of her control, there was no knowing what I would say or do that could jeopardise her very existence in this place. It seemed obvious to me that she would not take such a risk and that ultimately I would find my way into a grave next to Lorca.

Much as I fought against these feelings, knowing full well that they would undermine our relationship, they crept up on me no matter where I was or what I was doing. Even increasing my intake of red wine could not shut out my growing uneasiness about Eloïse because, no matter how I dressed it up, suspicion would turn to fear.

In turn, I began to watch Eloïse whenever the occasion presented itself. I never caught her watching me in the garden but the feeling of always being under observation became a fixture of my days. During our evenings together, I found myself searching for any nuance in her conversation or in her look that would confirm my growing fears. I found nothing. She remained her usual fascinating, gracious, attentive and considerate self. She was loving towards me, solicitous and caring and I felt so guilty at harbouring doubts about her, trying desperately not to give any signs of doing so. If it were possible, she seemed to be more romantic than before, wooing me in all sorts of imaginative ways, to the point where my obsessive suspicion of her motives almost started to diminish.

And then there was the accident.

In search of a means to distract my mind from my constant manic thoughts, I feared the secret garden as somehow the seat of my growing uneasiness. I could feel the panic building up in me. I was losing control of my thoughts; knew it but could do nothing about it. It was just the same as had happened at the time of the 'Event', a sort of mental helplessness when a hundred different thoughts flooded my brain while I seemed to be standing outside my body watching my mind losing control, unable to process any of those frightening, racing thoughts, desperate for them to stop. Instinctively, I felt the darkness descending on my soul.

Constantly, I looked behind me or scanned the shrubs around me, fearing imminent danger but not knowing why nor from whom. It felt that everyone was after me, but who was 'everyone' and why were they persecuting me?

The wine no longer seemed to help and for the first time since throwing away my medication, I regretted it. Even its zombie-like effect on me would be preferable to the frantic racing of my mind. Unable to keep still, I was moving about from place to place around the estate, through overgrown shrubbery and across old lawns whose long, knotted grass snagged my ankles. Eventually, I realised that I was at the lake, at the very place where I dragged Lorca's body out onto the bank – an area I had wanted to avoid at all costs. Vivid images of her swollen face flashed before me and I started to run. Somehow, I knew that I needed to keep moving, to keep running ahead of my thoughts. My only relief was in not keeping still long enough for the black thoughts to settle in my mind.

Finding myself at the old barn, I sought out the ancient motorbike and tinkered with it until, reluctantly, it stuttered into life. I pumped the oil piston near the tank and then coaxed it out towards the fields. It ran rough at first, finally settling down to a steady, if noisy, tick-over as the petrol swished around more in the tank.

At the top of the field, I opened the throttle and gradually picked up speed. The old feelings of exhilaration and total freedom surged through me. I never heard the tyre burst.

The handlebars were wrenched out of my hands as they turned at ninety degrees and the bike veered sharply to the right towards the rough ground at the end of the field. I'd forgotten that I had screwed open the hand throttle when I was trying to start it and now the engine was still racing although my hand was no longer on the throttle grip. I crashed along the rough ground, unable to steer with the front tyre flat.

I didn't see the hole. The front wheel dropped into it and the bike stopped dead as the engine stalled and I was pitched head first over the handlebars. All may have been well had I not had my instep and toes wedged under the front footrest and the rear brake pedal. I started a long, slow somersault and felt a sharp crack and stab of intense pain and knew instinctively that my foot was smashed even before I slammed into the ground, knocking all the wind out of my lungs.

I lay perfectly still on my back. Fortunately, the bike had stalled and with the front wheel locked into the rabbit hole had tilted over sideways and was no longer a threat. A sharp, throbbing, searing pain shot through my foot and by the time I'd unlaced my boot, my instep had ballooned to twice its normal size and there was blood where the laced leather had cut into it. Realising that I was quite unable to walk, I lay for a while, hoping that Eloïse was, somehow, aware of my accident and would appear and help me back to the house and then use her medical knowledge to look after me.

After what felt like a long time it seemed obvious that she was not coming. I could either stay there until she missed me and found me during her nightly prowls around the grounds or try to crawl back on my own. The thought of lying there for hours in the dark drove me to start the long, painful crawl home.

How long it took me to get back to the manor was impossible to say. The pain from my foot seemed to increase with every yard as I crawled forward. Fortunately, we never locked the doors and I finally dragged myself into the sitting room, long after darkness had fallen. Heaving myself onto the chaise longue, I called out repeatedly to Eloïse but with no result. I assumed that she was either in her bedroom in the derelict wing of the house, in the trance-like state that passed for sleeping in her world or, having missed me, was out in the grounds, sniffing me out. Pain notwithstanding, my exhaustion allowed me to fall into a fitful sleep.

When I awoke, after another bad dream about being watched, Eloïse was standing over me with a strange, fixed look on her face. She appeared to be listening to my garbled explanation of events but she did not react in any way and remained silently staring down at me. She had always been so gentle and solicitous towards me that her apparent indifference surprised me.

Like plenty of men, I sought female sympathy when hurt and injured and expected that she would automatically be my nurse as well as my lover and mate. Eloïse, however, extended no sympathy towards me at all, nor did she even say anything to me and remained looking down on me with a fixed stare and immovable expression.

I knew that I was injured entirely as a result of my own stupidity and that, in some ways, she had the right to be angry with me but I felt deeply hurt by her lack of any reaction to my obviously painful and helpless condition. I expected her to at least examine my foot and to know what to do. She could be infinitely gentle and she could have bandaged me up and made me as comfortable as possible while consoling me and murmuring words of sympathy. She was certainly capable of carrying me upstairs and laying me in my bed. Instead, she refused even to utter a word and seemed content to leave me sprawled on the chaise longue in the parlour.

She continued to stare at me, immovable and in total silence. Eventually, I concluded that she must be in some sort of fixed trance-like state that I hadn't seen before and I would just have to wait for her to come out of it. She would then, no doubt, be devastated at leaving me so long without her help.

Left to manage for myself, I did the best I could to get into a more comfortable position but my foot throbbed so much that I didn't know what to do to lessen the pain. Finally, exhausted, I slept and then awoke with a start to find Eloïse looking down on me still. The starlight at the window was reduced by dark clouds and I could only just make out her form against the dim light filtering into the room. She remained, as before, motionless and silent.

'Help me, Eloïse, please. I'm cold now. Why are you ignoring me? You've said nothing. Are you punishing me for something?'

There was no reply. The rigid stare did not flicker. This complete change in her left me totally dismayed. I wanted to embrace her and feel her hug me back as she always had before but I could not even put my foot to the floor to hop. Nothing I said produced the slightest reaction in her and the fixed stare seemed to become more and more malevolent. The pain was too much and I must have fallen asleep again.

When I awoke, it was daylight outside. I thought then that Eloïse would have gone to the darkness of her room and was surprised to find her still there, staring down on me. I called out to her but, as before, she did not move or answer me. I was hungry and very thirsty. My legs felt cold but my forehead was burning hot. I shivered and sweated at the same time. Once, I tried to get up, thinking that I might be able to hop about and find something to use as a crutch. When I swung my broken foot off the chaise and towards the floor, it throbbed horrendously, my head swam and I almost passed out. Before I managed to get my boot off, part of it had dug deep into my instep and there was blood everywhere.

Time passed very slowly but I fought against sleep, fearing that I would be asleep when Eloïse came out of her apparent trance. Shivering in the gloomy room in spite of the warm weather, I somehow passed the day and as soon as night showed at the window, I allowed myself to try to sleep. The pain had become a constant, dull ache and I was weak from lack of food and water and constant shivering.

It was dark when I awoke but, again, a small amount of starlight filtered into the room. Eloïse still stood over me, exactly as before, silent and unmoving. I think I may have been delirious because I can remember talking to her for a long time, even begging her to tell me what wrong I had done her to make her behave in such a cold way towards me. As far as I remember, she made no reply.

This scenario was repeated. I lost track of time and just remember periods of light and darkness. There was nothing to eat or drink and I had to urinate on the floor. My physical condition became increasingly disgusting to me. I had given up trying to get any sort of response from Eloïse and although she was always there in the room when I awoke, she was totally unresponsive, like a tailor's dummy.

How much time had passed since the accident, I had no way of knowing. During one period of consciousness, I realised that I no longer felt hungry or thirsty or hot or cold and I understood then that I was going to die. My life was slipping away and, as if in some sort of macabre sympathy, the room was decaying also. It seemed that everything, the furniture, the wallpaper, curtains, carpet, was rotting away. Even the long dress that the ever silent and motionless Eloïse was wearing began to fall into tatters.

I knew it would not be long now. Death was waiting patiently for me and I was surprised each time I awoke that I still lived. I lay in silence, waiting for sepsis to slip me into death.

Then, during a more lucid interval, I thought I heard an unfamiliar sound, not the scurry and pitter-patter of the rats but a crisp, metallic sound like the slamming of a car door. Presently, I heard a noise out in the passage that led to the front door. A voice called 'Hello?' and startled me. For some reason, I did not attempt to reply, as if the silence had been holding my world together and if I broke it, the shell I existed in might disintegrate.

Long moments passed and then, through my increasingly unfocused eyes, I thought I could discern a figure in the doorway. She started when she saw me, gasped and then stepped back. After a moment, a dusty torch beam fell on me and a voice said, 'Police. Don't be afraid. We're here to help you.'

In that moment, my delirious mind focused immediately. Dying was one thing, being found by the police was quite another. I thought of Eloïse, of Lorca and of myself. A young woman in uniform appeared and I could see the look of horror and disgust on her face.

I closed my eyes and let go.

CHAPTER 10

'So you will be delivered of the forbidden woman, from the foreign
woman with her smooth words, who forsakes the company of her
youth and forgets the covenant of her God; for her house sinks down
to death and her paths to the departed; none who go to her come
back, nor do they regain the paths of life.'
PROVERBS 2 V. 16–19 [HEBREW TRANSLATION]

BELLE'S DIARY

Last Entry. January 1973

In a way, I regret tearing up my story about witches, pixies
and elves. I'd thought to replace it with a children's book about
fairies and evil queens and then, in the back of my mind, I had
this idea of writing a book about witchcraft, my ancestors and
the power of 'white' magic. What put me off was the thought
of all that research into potions, herbs and natural medicines, to
say nothing of spells and incantations. I don't think I have the
tenacity for all that. Besides, it would take all the pleasure out of
it. And, anyway, it's all been done before.

Sally, my newspaper reporter friend, says that publishing is
an absolute cut-throat business anyway.

But, as I've always said, everything happens for a purpose. Although I didn't know it at the time, tearing up my manuscript was a good thing because now I can concentrate all my energy on this new venture.

Sally has loads of interesting stuff from her years of being a reporter but a lot of it is covered by confidentiality clauses imposed by the newspapers she worked for. So she's had this brilliant idea of collaborating with me, as a sort of proxy. She'll give me all the info and ghost write it with me but it will have my name on the cover. She chose me because we are old school friends but also, by one of those tricks of life that some people call coincidences, I happened to know the guy Jack who's the subject of her latest and easily most macabre report.

As I told Sally, I knew from the moment I set eyes on him that Jack was trouble. I even showed her the entries in my diary where I said as much. What a tremendous vindication of my powers and instincts – or whatever people want to call them! People round here are going to see me in a different light when this story comes out. I'll get the respect I deserve. Of course, there'll be money in it too. Mary-Jane for life!

Sally's given me loads of stuff that wasn't even in the newspapers and I've carefully compiled the facts ready for when we eventually collaborate on the book. I've had plenty of time for that because, of course, we had to wait until after the trial – or rather, I should say, hearing, since poor Jack was found unfit to plead, as they say.

Sally is worried that we might get in trouble by using some stuff from the coroner's report that could in some way be confidential and there's other 'official' stuff that might be subject to recent privacy laws and regulations. I'm not too bothered about that though because the book will be vetted before publication and anyway Jack is in no fit state to initiate legal proceedings against anybody. He's been sectioned and can't make any decisions for himself, even if he could ever think straight again. The publishers will see to all that.

So, I'm going to copy all my notes down here in case I mislay them or in case we aren't allowed to publish some of it after all.

My feelings about Jack that first time we met at the pub were correct. He was carrying a lot of emotional baggage and, as it turned out, that haunted look in his eyes was justified.

It came out, after his arrest, that he was already known to the police. About a year before he turned up here, he'd been arrested in London on suspicion of murder. Jacques Georges De Vere, his real name, was from an old and respected Anglo-French family. Born in London and educated at the Sorbonne in Paris, he eventually entered the family banking business and was sent to their London office. For a while, everything was fine. He had it all: good looks, impeccable manners, smart clothes, nice apartment and lots of money! Soon after his arrival in London, he found a girlfriend, Lindsey, and moved her into his flat.

It was the good life for Jacques, or Jack as he called himself in England: an endless round of smart parties, exotic holidays, weekends in European capitals, Prague, Budapest. Things were good too with Lindsey and he told his friends he considered her the woman of his dreams.

Soon, however, cracks began to appear. It seems that Jack, for all his good looks and charm, was not a gifted banker. His hedge fund suffered more than most from the bumpy financial climate of the recession and he didn't stand up well under pressure. Of course, Lindsey noticed it first. He developed many of the signs of depression and something of a persecution complex. He drank heavily and, steadily, his outgoing personality changed and he turned in on himself, analysing everything people said to him or the way they behaved in front of him.

Lindsey eventually became terrified of Jack, not because he ever hurt her or even threatened her in any way but because his paranoia became so great, even with the medication prescribed for him.

Jack promised to get help and started seeing a lady psychiatrist whom Lindsey described to friends as being 'exotic, foreign and rather scary herself'. Neither the medication nor the many hours he spent with this psychiatrist seemed to help; indeed his depression and especially his paranoia worsened. He believed that he was being followed and was convinced that he was being watched, spied on, that he lived in the constant presence of people whom he seemed to have invented himself in order to fulfil who knows what need in his psyche.

Eventually, together with his friends, Lindsey attempted to persuade Jack to enter a private clinic, a sanatorium really. He refused, of course, and the following day, Lindsey was found at the bottom of the stairs in the apartment she shared with Jack. Her neck was broken. There were no other marks of violence anywhere on her body and, as there was no sign of a forced entry and because Jack was the only other person there, he was naturally the prime suspect. He was arrested on suspicion of murder but had to be sectioned immediately and committed to the psychiatric wing of a prison.

The subsequent police investigation was in some difficulty. The coroner's report confirmed that there were no signs of violence anywhere on Lindsey's body and Jack had never been known to show any signs of the least violence towards her, nor anyone else for that matter, even in his most paranoid periods. There was nothing to suggest that it was not an accidental fall down the stairs and in fact one of her broken high heels was found on the landing.

Jack could not be questioned after being sectioned and, as far as the various doctors and psychiatrists were able to tell, he knew nothing about the incident. No one could find the slightest evidence that he and Lindsey had ever had any rows or rough patches in their relationship. The unanimous opinion was that Jack was infatuated with Lindsey and deeply – perhaps unnaturally deeply – in love with her. Her death was eventually ruled 'accidental' and the case against Jack quietly dropped.

He responded well to treatment, especially it seems from his lady psychiatrist, and he was eventually released into the 'custody' of family and friends who, having power of attorney, sold his London flat, invested some of the money to give him a small independent income (it being deemed that he could never return to his work in the City) and used the rest to buy him the cottage he moved into just a couple of miles outside this village.

It was at this time, when he started coming to the pub, that I first met him. It appears that Jack was very pleased with his new home and particularly with the garden. Manual work agreed with him. He was still on strong medication but it seems he was reluctant to take it because his mindset was still very fragile. Owing to his rather sheltered upbringing, he was incapable of looking after himself, so his guardians/trustees found a woman called Relorca whom they engaged as a sort of housekeeper/ minder and who was paid a good salary to keep a general eye on him and report to the trustees if he showed any signs of a relapse.

It seems that she was quite diligent in her duties but Jack was devious enough to conceal things from her. Whether he suspected that she was a part of his rehabilitation we will never know but he hid the fact that he was destroying his medication.

When he first came to the pub, I'm fairly sure he was accepted as quite normal by all the locals – everyone, that is, except me. I knew about these things. Anyway, *they* accepted him and, barring a certain reticence, he seemed sociable enough. One or two of the village girls, myself included, made a play for his attentions but he fended us off with such charm that we couldn't feel upset about it.

Aside from his rather vacant blue eyes, I noticed his heavy drinking and a fleeting look of alarm and suspicion when he was first approached by anyone. That is not to say that he wasn't good company and I spent several evenings with him in the pub and we laughed a lot, which is never a bad thing. There were clues though and, looking back on it, the first one was almost certainly the evening we had the 'clairvoyant'. (I put that word in parentheses because I don't believe in them at all and they have somehow become associated with my craft and that's not right at all.) Anyway, for some reason – perhaps to gratify his demons – Jack really wanted his fortune told. That's what it is, fortune telling. These people aren't mediums. That so-called clairvoyant woman ruthlessly used Jack to advertise her so-called powers by picking a fight with him, verbally. I very much doubt she had any idea of his vulnerability. It was pure coincidence and, as it happened, it was the worst thing she could have done to him in his condition. She drew everyone's attention to him, telling everyone he was 'evil', at a time when Jack just wanted to be accepted as normal and stay in the background.

Poor Jack! He was banished to the beer garden and though he tried to make a joke of it, it was plain that he was very upset. When I went outside to smoke a roll-up, he had moved to the far end of the garden and was seated in the darkest corner. He stayed there on his own while I was smoking and I fancied that I heard him talking to himself.

The barmaid told me that, before he left to walk home, Jack asked her the name of the woman he had been talking to but she had not seen anyone with him all evening. It was, after all, quite dark. None of this seemed important until after he was arrested.

Jack's Romanian housekeeper had disappeared and her family in Bucharest had alerted the police who in turn alerted the British authorities. The police in England had great difficulty in finding any trace of her after she stopped working at Jack's cottage. They must have sensed 'foul play' from the first because they searched his cottage and even dug up some of the garden.

It appears that, having failed to find Lorca, the police then concentrated on looking for her last employer, Jack. That too proved difficult. He seemed to have disappeared as well and though they questioned all the locals, they came no closer to locating him, a fact that made them even more inclined to believe he must be involved.

After several months of fruitless enquiry, it looked as though the trail had gone cold and the police resorted to putting up 'missing persons' flyers of both Lorca and Jack – something of a last-ditch attempt since it appears that they had already formed the opinion that the pair, for some reason, had run off together and the missing persons file was sent to the Paris police.

Of course, there is always an element of luck to investigation and, as chance would have it, one of the pub locals recalled seeing Jack come out of the overgrown lane leading to the old derelict White Lilies Manor after a most dreadful storm about a year before and thought it odd considering the place had been empty for as long as anyone could remember. Only the locals knew the place was there and most of them would avoid it at all costs because strange, dim lights had occasionally been glimpsed from across the surrounding fields. Even so, the police did not seem particularly interested until another local told them he'd seen a woman resembling the picture in the flyer walking along the road towards the pub but when he drove back a few minutes later, she had disappeared – so she either went into a nearby house or turned off at the lane to the manor. The place having been mentioned twice to the police, they decided it might be worth a look.

They were greeted by the most frightful scene when they finally entered White Lilies Manor.

Notes

Sally got the info on what happened at the house from her informant in the police who was present at the search. I don't know whether we will be able to use it or any of this next bit in the book in case it compromises the police officer and Sally herself. But I'll record it here anyway.

Search

The police arrived to search White Lilies at about mid-morning on 2 September 1972. It seemed a bit half-hearted, as searches go: only four uniformed PCs with a sergeant and an inspector.

At first, they were a bit daunted by the sheer size of both the house and the grounds and by the derelict, overgrown state of both. Even the path to the main entrance was covered with grass and the police vehicles could not go down as far as the manor.

What appeared to be the front door was unlocked, however, and partly ajar. Once inside the main passageway, the officers were each designated an area to search. Half the team were kept outside and sent around the sides and rear of the house in case anyone tried to leave at those points. In this, they were greatly hampered by dense undergrowth that came right up to the walls and the stagnant patches of water that were all that remained of the original moat.

Although it was still summer with fine, warm weather, 'Sheila', the WPC (not her real name), said she felt a chill in the house along with a strong smell of damp and decay and at once became uneasy and uncomfortable. Much to her dismay, each officer was to search separately, keeping in touch by radio. She got the distinct impression that the inspector, once he had seen the derelict state of the place, made up his mind that they weren't going to find anything there and that the whole thing was a wild goose chase. The PC with her was sent upstairs and she was left with the sergeant who opted to guard the door and told her to search the far end of the corridor leading into the gloomy depths of the house and then to enter any rooms she found on the way. She admitted to Sally later that she was quite nervous and glad to have the heavy torch she needed to light the windowless passage.

The room to her right appeared to have once been an extensive library. There were huge bookcases and hundreds of leather-bound mouldy books, a couple of heavy oak tables thick with dust and piles of fallen books and ceiling plaster on the damp carpet. The only window was half overgrown with ivy and honeysuckle outside and, here and there, the leaky ceiling had brought down some ornate cornice and wallpaper hanging in strips. Having shone her torch into all the dark recesses, Sheila was satisfied the place was empty and crossed the passage to enter the opposite room.

The door stood slightly ajar and she told Sally afterwards that she felt immediately disturbed and uneasy at the prospect of having to enter. The smell was different too: in addition to the musty smell of general decay and dampness, there was a distinct 'animal' odour. A sharp, acidic, foetid smell like the scent of a fox at the entrance to his earth and, at the same time, the smell of urine filtered out into the passageway.

Sheila approached warily, glancing over her shoulder in the vain hope that one of her colleagues might be nearby. She was quite alone. With a big sigh and great trepidation, she moved forward pushing the door open wider with her foot.

From what she could make out of the room, it was even more derelict than the library and appeared to be a sitting room or parlour. It was in half shadow but there was enough light to make out the bare walls with dirty square outlines where pictures had once hung. The pictures, with bits of fallen cornice and plaster, now littered the floor all over the musty, threadbare carpet.

Sheila hesitated. She instinctively knew that behind the half-open door, in the centre of the room was something she really didn't want to see. A step forward and the sweeping beam of her torch alighted on something that made her start back with a cry. She caught her breath and her heart thumped in her chest; there, in the circle of light cast by her torch, stood the figure of a woman, very tall, thin, in a long, old-fashioned dark dress, who remained completely motionless as Sheila slowly brought the beam of light up to her face. Huge, black, sightless eyes stared back, unblinking. Her long, black, almost waist-length hair was sprinkled with layers of dust and a pale, triangular, haunting face stared back at her, a cobweb over one gaunt cheek.

It took Sheila several seconds to recover her composure and to realise that she was staring at a mannequin, a shop model, decked out in a wig and heavy make-up, white powder, dark eyebrows and bright red lipstick.

Sheila edged cautiously forward for a closer look and was immediately aware of another presence. Hesitantly edging round the open door, she scanned the rest of the room.

The French windows to the back garden were partly obscured by heavy curtains, cobwebbed and faded, and the overgrowth covered the outside of the leaded panes. Various old-fashioned wooden side tables were scattered around and on one an old wind-up gramophone stood, its horn draped with cobwebs. Here and there, dusty oil lamps, their glass shades covered in soot, stood forlornly.

None of this mattered to Sheila because her eyes were drawn to the chaise longue in the centre of the room. In the gloom, she could just make out a reclining shape on the old, torn chaise, feet towards her, as she automatically swept her torch beam up until it caught the glint of two blue eyes. She jumped back into the doorway but kept her light focused on the dark form stretched out on the tatty upholstery.

This was no mannequin, no dummy in period clothes; this was a man looking back at her and blinking in the torchlight. She stood frozen to the spot but the form on the chaise moved and as it did so the foetid smell of unwashed human body wafted towards her. The torch beam fell on the man's feet and she could see that a shoe was missing and the foot swollen to twice the size of the other.

Suddenly, Sheila's voice came back. She moved the torch light back up to the man's face and he stared back. The growth of stubble on his face was becoming a beard and it, and the darkness, obscured his features enough for her to have to ask if he was Jack. The 'Yes' response was weak and hoarse. Pressing the transmit button on her collar radio, Sheila reported her findings and asked for an ambulance to be called. She then waited patiently for her colleagues. The sergeant arrived first and then the inspector. All three officers, overcoming their distaste at the smell, approached the chaise and, having compared Jack's face to the one on their poster, the inspector formerly told him that he was under arrest, cautioned him and noted the time. He was careful not to be specific about the charges and said only that it was in connection with the disappearance of Lorca Demetriu. In any case, Jack made no reply.

It being obvious that their prisoner was quite unable to abscond, the police then withdrew to a less odorous distance and the inspector mumbled a reluctant 'Well done' to Sheila.

Sally told me that this 'Sheila' was actually quite traumatised by the condition Jack was in and by the terrible state of the house that had obviously been derelict for years and was little short of a ruin.

It seemed very likely that if Jack had not been found by them, he would have been dead within a few days, probably from sepsis. As it was, he was in a serious condition, desperately dehydrated and had not eaten for more than a week.

As a 'reward' for finding Jack, Sheila was given the job of accompanying him to hospital. At first she had little to do but within a few days he had recovered surprisingly well and, with his damaged foot set and put in an air boot, was partly mobile and able to care for his appearance and wear some of the clothes provided.

Sheila had been told to write down everything he was able to tell her. This was not an official tape-recorded interview – that would come later and be carried out by senior officers of the CID – but rather an informal chat to gather facts to help these future interrogating officers. Sheila wasn't really very pleased about that but, without her notes, Sally and I would be in the dark when we come to write our book.

Armed with a notepad and forms, Sheila was granted the use of a private room near the hospital ward and was surprised to find Jack sitting quietly there, looking clean, smart and relaxed. This initial scenario turned to disappointment when she came to realise the difficulty of the task confronting her. Jack, though recovered physically, was in a dreadful state mentally. He would, she knew, in due course be seen by psychiatrists but she soon discovered that even the simplest questions were beyond his ability to respond in an intelligent way.

Jack, a man she had been told was well educated and cultured, required a different approach. In the afternoon, she changed to a more informal chat, laid back and friendly.

At first, this produced results in that Jack seemed more rational. They spoke about his injured foot and how it happened and even tried to work out how long he had been helpless in that awful room before she had found him. Gradually, Sheila, a trained interviewer before joining the police, brought the conversation round to matters more related to her enquiries.

In spite of the uncomfortable fact that he was the prime suspect in Lorca's disappearance, Sheila found herself beginning to like Jack. Shaved, showered and re-clothed, he brushed up rather well, she thought, and his attractive smile made her feel she was talking to an old friend instead of a suspect.

About half an hour into the interview, everything changed. Sheila was called out of the room to receive the news that what was believed to be Lorca's body had been found in a shallow grave in the manor grounds. She should then have terminated the interview but as she considered it an 'informal chat', she pressed on avoiding any mention of Lorca and the gruesome find in the sunflower patch.

How long, she asked Jack, had he been living in White Lilies Manor? When he replied that it was more than a year, she found that difficult to believe.

'But it's completely derelict, Jack… uninhabitable…'

'Derelict?' he replied with a look of complete surprise. 'Derelict? No. A bit old-fashioned, I'll admit, but we liked it that way.'

Sheila had been wondering how anyone could possibly consider the manor anything other than a damp, crumbling, musty ruin of a building but picked up on the last words Jack had said. 'We?' Jack did not respond and she prompted, '*We*, Jack?' He stared at the floor, obviously uneasy. 'Come on, Jack. Are you saying that you weren't on your own? Are you talking about Lorca?'

'Yes. She was with me at the cottage…' He replied evasively.

'No, Jack, we were talking about the manor. Who else was there with you?'

This direct probing was counterproductive and he clammed up immediately. Sheila decided on a different approach.

'There were lots of women's clothes there, Jack, at the manor, I mean, old-fashioned long dresses and big hats. Whose were those? Were they there when you moved in, along with the mannequin in the long dark wig?'

Those last few words touched a nerve and he looked up, eyes flashing with anger.

'Mannequin?' he shouted. 'There was no mannequin!'

Sheila pressed her apparent advantage.

'You know, Jack, the shop dummy standing by the chaise longue where we found you…'

He jumped up from his chair, wincing with pain, stared at Sheila and then shouted at her, 'Don't talk about her like that!'

This outburst brought a nurse into the room followed by the uniformed police officer who was on guard outside. Jack was led out, staring back at poor Sheila.

She told us later that she had not felt afraid of him, only a deep sadness at his confused mental state and frustration because she believed she was starting to get somewhere with her probing.

The coroner's report on Lorca's post-mortem is a legal document available in the public domain, so Sally thinks we will be allowed to publish it – or parts of it – in our book. It contained only a couple of findings seemingly relevant to our account. The first was that Lorca had died instantly from a broken neck; the only other physical injuries being some peculiar small grazes on her throat just under her chin. She had not been sexually assaulted. The second was that her body had been immersed in water for at least a week before being buried where it was later found. In the entire report, there was nothing to indicate her possible killer.

Sheila was present at Jack's subsequent interviews with a team of three psychiatrists and the notes she took pretty much summed up their findings. The exact nature of his psychological illness was discussed in great detail at his unfit-to-plead hearing; it was complicated and long-standing. Sheila's notes were able to shed some light on Jack's existence at the manor and are summarised as follows:

For some reason, Jack believed that he had been appointed gardener at the manor, though how he found the place and what drew him there and led to that belief was never established and he remained stubbornly silent on those points. He moved in and lived in absolute squalor. He did not see it that way, however, and the derelict, rambling house appeared to him as merely 'a bit old-fashioned'. He remained there undetected for well over a year, regardless of the fact that all utility services had long since been cut off and the place was damp and rat-infested. The only witnesses who saw him during that time were the locals at the pub, myself included, and we can testify that he appeared always clean and well turned out, which is surprising under the circumstances.

The most revealing and worrying facts were supplied by Jack himself though they had to be drawn out of him with great patience over many hours of psychoanalysis.

It appears that Jack believed himself to be deeply in love with a woman he called Eloïse. She was his dream woman in every way and he described, unwillingly, their relationship as blissful and their life together at the manor as the happiest time of his life. He was very defensive about this Eloïse and appeared to be deeply concerned for her welfare. He was very careful in what he said about her but the psychiatrists formed the opinion that he believed there was something very exceptional about her and that she was most unusual in many ways. There was, however, apart from the women's clothes, no trace of any other person having lived at the manor for years.

There seemed to be a definite block in Jack's mind that made him very reluctant to discuss 'Eloïse' but at the same time it became clear that he had felt 'betrayed' by her at the time he was discovered. Eventually, he revealed that 'Eloïse' had not helped him after he broke his foot and instead had stood over him, watching him silently. When questioned further about her or the mannequin in his room, he clammed up immediately.

Gradually the depth of Jack's fantasy world at the manor was revealed and it became clear that his mind was deeply disturbed, with his refusal to take any medication and heavy drinking leading to a total breakdown.

The circumstances of Lorca's death, particularly her broken neck, led the police to look again at the circumstances surrounding the death of Jack's girlfriend Lindsey two years previously. The results were, again, inconclusive.

Notes on the fit-to-plead hearing

Sally and I both went to the pre-trial hearing. The defence maintained that Jack's mental condition rendered him unfit to plead. The psychiatrists confirmed that to be the case, even the one called by the prosecution.

The Crown seemed content to dispense with the cost of a long trial and more or less let it be known that they expected Jack to be sent to a mental prison facility 'At Her Majesty's Pleasure', as they say. So this hearing was something of a formality – going through the motions. Justice had to be seen to be done. Jack was legally represented but no one from his family was there. It was very boring stuff. Various reports on Jack's condition were read out but, as the prosecution and defence were in agreement, it was all something of a foregone conclusion.

The final witness was the psychiatrist who attended Jack during his first breakdown – the 'Event' as he apparently called it – and who was caring for him right up to the time he disappeared from the cottage.

The court fell silent when she entered and Jack, who had taken absolutely no interest in all that had gone before, suddenly seemed to wake from his trance-like state and became suddenly very attentive and agitated.

Never have I seen a more striking and unusual woman! Her considerable height was accentuated by her ultra slim figure, a sort of cross between a ballet dancer and an athlete

– perhaps a swimmer. An extremely pale complexion clashed with the tight, black jacket and pencil skirt she was wearing. Her triangular face was framed by a mane of long, black hair and she wore, with the exceptional permission of the judge, large dark glasses.

When she addressed the court, in a deep, cultured voice, she gave her name as Dr Maria Zaleska – or some such Slavic name, and in slightly accented English confirmed her professional role as psychiatrist. She smiled, only once, at the judge, revealing big white teeth in a large but attractive mouth.

Jack's legal team walked her through her evidence, asking her only to try to avoid the use of complicated medical terms in her replies. In short, she confirmed that Jack was suffering from a very severe delusional illness and that this condition, serious as it was, had been greatly aggravated by his refusal to take his prescribed medication. She concluded that, in her professional opinion, Jack lived in his own delusional world and could not be held responsible for his actions nor distinguish between right and wrong in the legal definition of those terms. Nor, she insisted, could anything he said have any credence whatsoever. She finished speaking and then, to his obvious discomfort, stared at the judge with her huge black eyes, under dark, slanting eyebrows. His Lordship seemed strangely uneasy but, finally, tearing his eyes away, appeared to pull himself together.

Dr Zaleska was then dismissed, thanked by the judge and rose to leave the court without even a backward glance at poor Jack who had remained deeply disturbed throughout her presence. I could feel the intensity of her eyes on me as she passed; an intense, inexplicable feeling of uneasiness overcame me and a shiver ran up my spine. Not a sound could be heard in court. A strange, musky odour lingered on the air.

About the Author

Only with the passing of time and the current less hostile attitude towards psychosis and the supernatural, has Count Collin Van Reenan felt able to tell his story, recounted in *The Spaces in Between*. After the events recounted in the book, Collin returned to England and for many years worked as a police officer both in London and in Paris, and then as an interpreter/translator for the Home Office, the police, and the courts of law, mainly Bow St. and the Old Bailey. Before that, he worked in many jobs including being an interpreter at the Old Bailey trial for the murder of Victoria Climbié and the 'body in the suitcase' murder in York. *Dinner with Eloïse* is his second book.

Acknowledgements

Many thanks to Heather Boisseau, Clare Christian, and Lizzie Lewis at RedDoor; to Sue Jeffery who deciphered my scrawl to type the manuscript; to Patrick Knowles for his beautiful cover design; to Lady Polly Aldous for her continuing support; and to Norman Holland for his long-standing friendship and encouragement.

ALSO BY COUNT COLLIN VAN REENAN

'An utterly captivating curiosity'
CAROLINE SMAILES

COUNT COLLIN VAN REENAN

THE
SPACES
IN BETWEEN

BASED ON A TRUE STORY

Preface

*'This is one of those cases in which the imagination is
baffled by the facts.'*

WINSTON CHURCHILL

My name is Marie–Claire Gröller, Doctor of Psychiatry.
I deal with the neurotic, the psychotic and even the
psychopathic, and I have many strange tales to tell; but none
so utterly mysterious as the facts related in the following pages.

Normally (not a word that figures often in my profession),
the rules of patient confidentiality would prevent such a story
from ever leaving my files. There are, however, exceptions. In
the case of dire need of the patient and with his full consent, it
may be permitted to publish such details in the desperate hope
that it may bring relief and closure for him.

In this case the patient is, moreover, also my friend.

His steadily deteriorating condition has forced me to
take these unusual steps. Someone, somewhere, knows what
happened, and could, if he or she had the courage to come
forward, bring some sort of respite to a man who has suffered
a great wrong and who is slowly sinking under the despair of
not knowing why.

I first met the man (whom I shall call Nicholas) in late
October 1968. After I qualified from the Sorbonne in Paris and
spent two years at the Pitié-Salpêtrière Hospital, in 1968 my

parents helped me to open my own practice in a small town called Rueil-Malmaison, about fifteen minutes by car from the centre of Paris to the north-west, across the Seine and behind the beautiful Bois de Boulogne park. The town was already well served by consultants in all aspects of medicine, and at first I struggled to find work. Patients are most often referred to psychiatrists by general practitioners, and they preferred established and experienced colleagues. There was also, at that time, a certain amount of prejudice against women in the medical profession.

Fortunately, a young doctor close to my own practice was very helpful to me (we later married) and sent me my first patient.

My father was a *commissaire de police*, a high rank in the *police judiciaire*, and used part of his retirement pension to set me up in practice. My *cabinet* or practice was rather humble, consisting simply of two rooms above a lingerie boutique on the Rue Paul Vaillant-Couturier, a few yards from the church where the Empress Joséphine is entombed. The first room, furnished only with a desk and filing cabinet, served as the reception, and the second, with just two armchairs and a small table, as my practice room. I had to act as my own receptionist and answer the telephone to make appointments.

It was nearly a week before I received my first call. Dr David wished to refer a young man. The patient claimed he was suffering from insomnia, but the doctor suspected he was in fact clinically depressed. This young man, who lived nearby, was not registered locally with any doctor and had asked Dr David merely for a prescription for sleeping tablets. However, his appearance, lack of appetite and general state of health suggested to the good doctor that the problem was in the mind rather than the body. Dr David warned me that, although his new patient had reluctantly agreed to see me, he was very reticent and wary when asked about his background.

Trying not to sound too eager, I arranged an appointment, and 10 a.m. the next day found me peeping surreptitiously through the blinds on the street side of my rooms. When the bell sounded, I felt a childlike and inappropriate excitement, and wondered if perhaps I should be consulting someone myself!

Heart racing, I admitted my first private patient and led the way upstairs.

It was only when we found ourselves next to my two armchairs that I really had a chance to look at my client. He waited politely for me to sit, and that gave me a chance to observe him. My first impressions were of a man about twenty-three or twenty-four years of age, of medium height and build. I also noted that he was wearing an expensive, elegant if rather shabby dark grey suit, beautifully cut but in a rather old-fashioned double-breasted style, which seemed to hang on him as though he had lost some weight since it was made. Unusually for the times, his hair was short – brown, wavy, but with some premature greying at the sides. The shape of his face, together with his fair complexion, suggested that he was a northern European. His deep-set grey eyes were ringed with dark shadows that suggested lack of sleep.

Uneasy at my perhaps too obvious scrutiny, he fidgeted, eyes on the floor; but then he looked up suddenly with a shy smile and I glimpsed – again unusually for those heavy-smoking, coffee-drinking times – perfect white teeth.

Introducing myself and explaining Dr David's concern, I asked him outright if anything was troubling him. He fidgeted uneasily again and refused to meet my eyes. Finally, he said that he was unable to sleep well, following an 'unsettling experience' a few months previously. His appetite also seemed to have deserted him and he felt unable to relax. He lived alone and was currently unemployed, living on an allowance sent to him by his parents.

As I listened to his soft voice, I noted that his French was clear and his pronunciation precise – an educated French that was, I thought, very good. In fact too good; I was listening to someone who was not speaking his mother tongue. I looked again at the name on the file I had just created – 'Nicholas Van R.' – and assumed that I was dealing with a Belgian, from Flanders. When I enquired, however, he told me that he was in fact English, though his mother was Irish and his father's family had connections in South Africa.

I continued to probe and learned that he had come to Paris aged thirteen because his mother wanted him to be educated in France. At first he had boarded at the Lycée Henri-IV, afterwards spending a couple of years at the University of Liège, Belgium, where he had relatives, and then about two years ago had started a humanities course at the Sorbonne, with the intention of becoming a journalist. The first year, he had studied existentialism under Professor Paul Genestier, whom he greatly admired, but in his second year his tuition was taken over by Professor Robert S.– H.–, who, although he treated him well, was not someone Nicholas had been able to warm to.

He stopped suddenly and looked up at me; again that shy smile.

'You were going to tell me about your "unsettling experience"…' I prompted.

'Well…' He hesitated. 'I'm not actually sure it's relevant…'

'Please go on.' I smiled back. I could see we were getting closer to the problem and I needed to keep the momentum going.

He was uncomfortable now and again refused to look at me. When he was not smiling, his face appeared gaunt, and the dark shadows around his eyes made him look older than his years.

'Please… Nicholas, if I may call you that… I can't help you if you don't explain…'

Slowly, he began to resume his story.

Collin Van Reenan

'Well, it all started to go wrong – for me, that is – just at the start of January of this year. My parents retired to South Africa, but for some complicated reason their bank accounts were frozen… some business court case, I was told. Suddenly, my allowance stopped. I didn't have much in the way of savings but I found some evening work as a *plongeur* in various restaurants and was just about managing… by making all sorts of economies. But…'

He looked up at me.

'But I didn't have a work permit and, when my student visa expired in March, I didn't have the funds to show to get it renewed. I was unhappy with my classes… I hadn't taken to Professor S.– H.–, as I said, and I had problems meeting my rent. The final straw was the outbreak of the student riots in May. There was a lot of damage… the restaurants closed and I could no longer earn money. I lost my rooms and had to doss down with friends… I even stayed with the Professor, just for a few days, that's how desperate I was. I think I lived on *cafés au lait* for a couple of weeks. Then –'

He stopped abruptly, and it was obvious that he was approaching something that made him uncomfortable.

'Please go on, Nicholas. I'm here to listen.'

He looked hard at me, as if trying to decide whether he could trust me, looked down at the floor and then, very slowly, raised his eyes to mine, made his decision and began, haltingly, 'Then Bruno… a friend… found an ad in *Le Figaro*… for an English tutor… to live in. It seemed the only answer… the police were after me for overstaying my visa – you know, they threw all the foreign students out after the riots. Well, anyway, I took the job… in this really strange house… with an even weirder family.'

He stopped again and I was shocked to see tears running down his face.

– 187 –

'And then – then that's when it started.'

He stopped, unable to speak, and to hide his embarrassment stared rigidly at the floor. It was obvious to me that if I pressed him further it would only be detrimental to his confidence.

After a while, I said gently, 'Look, Nicholas, I hope to be able to help you but I need to know the full details. I can't promise you a "quick fix" but we have plenty of time. I'd like you to make another appointment to continue our chat –'

'I don't think I can talk about it, doctor...' he broke in, agitated. 'It's too long and complicated and you won't believe me anyway – no one does.'

I could see there was no point in continuing right now, so I suggested a tried and tested, if unimaginative, approach.

'Well, Nicholas, we will meet again next week, and in the meantime I would like you to write down all the details. Write it *all* down. It's important that you don't leave anything out. Do you understand?'

He nodded without looking up.

'Now, has Dr David given you any medication?'

He shook his head.

'OK. I'm going to prescribe something for you, just a mild sedative, but you must try to eat regularly and get plenty of exercise and fresh air. Do we have a deal?'

He smiled a little sadly and stood up, thanking me.

From the window, I watched him leave the building and wander down the street in the direction of the church.

My first patient. I knew it was going to be quite a challenge, but nothing could have prepared me for what eventually followed.

Suddenly, my practice took off. In the week following that first session with Nicholas, I had a consultation practically every day, and I confess that I gave little thought to his case. So when he turned up the following Friday I had to consult my notes hurriedly before I called him through.

He looked tired and drawn, and once again ill at ease. It occurred to me that there must be a woman involved in this, perhaps unrequited love; but, whatever it was, I suspected that having a woman as his psychiatrist might be something he was finding difficult.

The battered folder he put down in front of me looked suspiciously thin for a summary of his 'unsettling experiences' over a period of almost six weeks, and I began to doubt the wisdom of asking him to write them down. Perhaps a series of interview sessions would have induced him eventually to be more forthcoming.

I made no comment, though, and took the folder with good grace. As I looked up suddenly, I caught him looking at me, studying me, as it were, as though trying to make up his mind to trust me. It convinced me even more that there was a woman at the bottom of all this – '*cherchez la femme*', as we say. He smiled to hide his embarrassment at being caught out, and I felt instinctively that I had passed some sort of a test for him, perhaps by not commenting on the brevity of the folder, and that he accepted me. It was a turning point in our relationship and I hoped his newfound trust would help him open up to me.

The manuscript was a huge disappointment. Even a cursory glance proved that. A series of dates and a short recounting of 'facts'; it was just like a police witness statement – a report of an incident, ten pages of facts with no feeling, no personal observation, nothing at all to help me.

Deciding to test his confidence in our relationship, I pointedly closed the file, looked up at him and held his eyes, forcing him to look at me.

'I'm sorry, Nicholas; this is not at all what I had in mind. It's a legal dossier – a list of events; I want to know how you *felt*, what you thought, how you reacted. I want a blow-by-blow account of your emotions, your intimate perception of these events…'

He looked shocked that I should suggest such a thing.

'Nicholas, I need to see inside your head. I'm a mind doctor, not a mind-reader: I can't guess how you felt then, or feel now. You have to *tell* me. You said you wanted to be a writer, so use your talent, Nicholas, and don't come back till you've written it all down for me.'

I knew it was a calculated risk; he might not come back at all. But I had to take a chance on that, or I could not help him.

I did not see Nicholas for several weeks. Nobody did. He locked himself away in his tiny flat in Rueil-Malmaison and – he told me later – just wrote and wrote until he had it all down on paper.

When he delivered it, his physical appearance so shocked me that I sent him back to Dr David for an urgent check-up; I thought he might be suffering from exhaustion. He was eventually persuaded to join some friends on a short trip to Italy.

It took me several hours to read Nicholas's account, and it had a profound effect on me. At first, I thought it a romance, and then perhaps a crime thriller and, finally, a ghost story.

It follows here, in its entirety, with no changes except the correction of a few archaic grammatical expressions and slightly old-fashioned idioms. His French also contains one or two student slang expressions that I have changed to avoid confusion. Throughout his account, Nicholas has varied people's first names, sometimes using the French form, that is, Natalie, and sometimes the Russian, Natalya; likewise Serge and Sergei. I have seen no point in standardising these, as the sense is always evident. When unusual Russian words have been used, an explanation is given.

It is a strange and harrowing story.

CHAPTER 1

Unrest

'Ce n'est pas une révolution, Sire, c'est une mutation.'

SLOGAN, MAY 1968

The few francs that I had were long since spent and a Métro ticket was out of the question; so when the tube stopped at Place Saint Michel I dodged the automatic barrier by going through behind another student, glued to his back and barging him forward so as not to get caught in the closing door. He knew but he didn't even turn round; I mean, we all did it in those days.

My mind was buzzing as we trooped up the steps of the exit. What would it be like, the Boulevard Saint Michel, after nearly two weeks of student riots? Would the trees still be standing? Would the fountain be running? Would all the shop windows be smashed?

I was so lost in thought that I didn't see him until it was too late and he'd seen me first. To go back down would have been too obvious, so I kept on up the steps and tried to look casual.

He was a few years older than I; twenty-six or twenty-eight perhaps, short hair, clean-shaven and wearing a very smart dark suit. It was a fine spring day in mid-May and the sun shone on the last few steps. But I felt a sudden chill.

I tried not to make eye contact but I could feel him looking at me, and when I came level with him on the top step he pushed his police ID right into my face. *'Police nationale, monsieur. Sûreté. Renseignments Généraux!'* He paused for effect and then spat out the words, *'Pièces d'identité. PAPIERS!'*

Police checks were nothing new to me; unused to such things at home in England, I had at first found them daunting, but as a student in Paris I had soon become inured to the process. But today I was afraid. Afraid because my visa had expired, afraid because I had no money, and afraid because the police were far from happy with students.

'Bonjour, Monsieur l'Inspecteur,' I stammered, and made a gesture as if to search my pockets for the sacred 'papers'. I needed to explain my situation as quickly as possible. *'Vous voyez, monsieur, le problème, c'est que –'*

I didn't get a chance to finish. The back of his hand hit me smack on the left cheek and I staggered back, blinking, nearly falling back down the steps to the Métro.

'Papiers, et que ça saute!' He hissed. Papers, and jump to it!

I thought of hanging a right hook on his chin and dismissed the idea instantly; even if I survived the subsequent beating, French prisons are hell. So I said nothing and did not resist as he dragged me across the pavement to the *'panier à salade'* parked in the nearby Rue de la Huchette. The van was already half full; a few *clochards* (tramps) and the rest students like me. Some bore the marks of earlier encounters, and I thought myself lucky to get off with just a hard slap – so far at least. Conversation was forbidden and shortly after, we were driven to the *commissariat* of the IVème *arrondissement*, across the river on the right bank, and 'interviewed' there.

I got lucky: my interviewer was an old inspector who I guessed was already retired and had been brought back to help out during this time of unrest. He had nothing to prove and had long since had his fill of violence; more to the point, he had spent some time in London and was something of an Anglophile, so I told him everything – the truth. It wasn't complicated: how I came to be there, where I was studying, what I was studying. Then I explained that my funds had been held up and that I couldn't find work because of the student riots. I assured him that it was only temporary and that I would soon receive some money and renew my student visa… basically, anything I thought might help my case.

I thought he seemed sympathetic, but my hopes came crashing down when he said they were taking me to the Gare du Nord and would put me on a train back to Calais and then England. But, when I got into the car, he sort of winked at me. At the station, he took me to the platform and on to the Calais train and then turned, looked hard at me, and walked away.

It took several seconds for it to dawn on me, and then I wasted no time in getting off the train and walking back into the station to lose myself in the crowds. This time I walked to Saint Michel and, after checking that the police control was no longer in place, cut off down the side streets to the little café we all frequented.

The walk was depressing: beautiful trees had been felled across the Boul'Mich and dozens of street-sweepers were out clearing the broken glass from the shop windows. Some of the barricades had not yet been dismantled, and here and there small groups of helmeted CRS in their long black rubber coats stood chatting and smoking. In one or two places I caught a whiff of tear gas, and there were blood spatters on the pavements.

The café appeared to be closed. There were no lights on and the windows were completely obscured by condensation. The door opened, though, and I saw Max and Aurélie sitting in the corner. Apart from them, the place was empty, the chairs piled upon the tables, the floor unswept and littered with dog-ends. Behind the counter, Jean-Marie nodded a greeting and a flick of his eyebrows asked the question.

'I've no money, Jean-Marie,' I said. '*Que dalle!*' Broke.

He shrugged and set the coffee machine in motion.

Max kept his eyes closed as I sat down. Aurélie looked up briefly and then went back to rolling a cigarette, one of the thin, dark tobacco ones wrapped in liquorice paper that she smoked endlessly. We had had a bit of a 'thing' going once, for a short time, a while before. She was quite attractive in a bohemian way, slim, with elfin features and short blonde hair.

But Aurélie wasn't interested in how she looked. She didn't need to attract a man – she was married to the Revolution – a sort of sixties version of the women who knitted while the heads from the guillotine rolled into the basket. She mumbled endlessly about student power, people power, the Left, Jacques Sauvageot, Alain Geismar, Daniel (Dany le Rouge) Cohn-Bendit; she knew them all, or so she said. She was really a doctor's daughter from Saint-Germain-en-Laye and was in revolt about that, along with everything else. This morning she looked terrible: great dark lines under her eyes, her hair matted and uncombed and her pretty, even teeth stained by nicotine and black coffee. She was wearing a shapeless pink woollen dress pulled in by a wide belt and with a huge, baggy rolled collar.

I leaned across the table and kissed her on each cheek but she didn't look up, and I noticed that she had been neglecting her personal hygiene as much as her appearance. Still, she droned on about the Revolution, the CRS, Fouchet and the Gaullists – a never-ending monologue that did not require any input from me, or anyone else for that matter. Just as well, because French politics left me cold. I just couldn't get excited about it all; these people were obsessed with revolutions and they kept restoring the 'Old Order' so they could have another revolution to replace it. I mean, five republics should be enough for anyone! It was a national pastime that I just could not get enthusiastic about.

Jean-Marie came over to our table carrying a huge bowl of milky coffee and a croissant to break into it. I'd been living on this stuff for nearly a week.

'I've no money,' I said again, but he just shrugged and slammed it down in front of me. That was the ambivalence of the Parisians – mean to the last centime of a bill, generous to a fault the next moment.

Max opened his eyes and looked up at me, at the coffee, at Aurélie, and then closed his eyes again and shrank lower into the duffel-coat arrangement that he lived in. His life veered from intense, almost frenetic energy to total lethargy. He could sleep almost anywhere and made a most unlikely *carabin*, or medical student. He had an astute brain, though, and could often beat me in a discussion. He was usually in funds, but he didn't offer it around.

So there we sat. No other customers. It was so quiet. The felled trees kept the Boul'Mich and the Boulevard Saint-Germain barred to traffic, and few people ventured out through the debris of the previous night's riots.

I closed my eyes and drifted off for a few seconds, to the accompaniment of Aurélie's monologue and the slight wheezing noise coming from Max's open mouth.

The slamming of the door and a gust of fresh air woke me in time to see Bruno's huge frame ambling towards us, lugging a battered suitcase that I realised, with foreboding, was mine. He greeted Aurélie with a kiss, took a look at the still-sleeping Max and, sitting down, stored the suitcase under the table and shook hands with Jean-Marie and myself, all in a series of high speed manoeuvres. Then he grinned at me.

I liked Bruno the best of all my student friends, a huge,

bluff, easy-going lad 'of peasant stock' as they say. But what he may have lacked in sophistication he made up for with his frank and open disposition. Engineering was his passion, but for some reason he preferred the company of humanities students and had attached himself to us within days of arriving in Paris from his home village near Metz. Bruno was a thoroughly decent guy and had allowed me to sleep on the couch in his room for the last week or so. So why the suitcase?

'Want the good news or the bad news?' He continued to grin.

'It's *all* bad, isn't it?'

'Not at all, Nico, old son. The bad bit is that you've got to vacate my room. The landlord's found out about it and he's threatening to chuck me out.'

I stared at him as my sluggish brain took in this latest disaster. Finally, I asked, 'So what's the good news?'

'I've found you a job, or sort of…'

Max opened his eyes and asked, 'A job? What, Nico?'

Bruno nodded, pleased with the reaction he was getting. From deep inside his coat, he extracted a crumpled scrap of paper and slapped it down on the table, where it proceeded to soak up the slops of Aurélie's spilled coffee. Snatching it up again, Bruno smoothed it carefully on a dry corner of the table and then pushed it over to me.

It appeared to be a blurry photocopy of the employment page of *Le Figaro*. Halfway down one column, an inch of print had been circled with a red pen. Bruno jabbed a thick finger at it excitedly. 'There, it's you to a T, Nico! Could solve all your problems, *mon pote.*'

Aurélie snatched it up and read it out loud. '*Native English-speaker wanted to tutor 17-year-old at home three days per week. Must speak French. Knowledge of Russian useful. Three months' renewable contract, board and lodging, generous salary.*'

I stared at Bruno. 'What on earth…?'

'No, listen, Nico. Think about it for a moment. Board and lodging, right? Generous salary, right? Native English-speaker, must speak French, right?'

'And Russian, Bruno, what about that?'

'You speak Russian, Nico. I heard you with that bloke who lives next to me…'

'That's Polish, and anyway, it's only a few phrases I picked up…'

'Nah, Nico, you speak *all* the languages – that's what you do, isn't it? Listen, it's only for three months. Somewhere to sleep, something to eat, better pay than washing-up, loads of spare time to study. And you won't miss much at the Sorbonne: it's all closed up now and it will be at least a couple of months before things get back to normal. Plus the fact that you'll be out of the way of the police checks, and then you can use your saved earnings when you apply for a new student visa.'

I opened my mouth to object, but then closed it again. What Bruno was saying actually made good sense and I didn't know why I was so reluctant to admit it.

Bruno's enthusiasm seemed suddenly to desert him and I felt that my ingratitude had hurt him. I couldn't even offer him a cup of coffee.

Aurélie, rolling yet another cigarette, looked up at me, questions written all over her face. Max, eyes still closed, said, 'Bruno's got a point. Sounds ideal to me.'

All of them were right. I realised that. They weren't just winding me up. It did make sense. I was just reluctant to admit it. I looked at the ad again. A seventeen-year-old; that might not be so bad – I mean, it wasn't as though it was a naughty young kid. Three months wasn't so long either, and it would be nice to have somewhere to sleep properly. The food would probably be what the family ate themselves, and few Parisians ate badly. Maybe I could bullshit the Russian language bit.

'OK, I'll give it a go. Where is it?' I said, more out of bravado than confidence. 'Neuilly! Christ! That's a good Métro ride away and, anyway, I haven't got any money.'

Bruno grinned again.

'Thought of that,' he said, holding up a 'Pasteur' – a five-franc note.

I took the note, and promised to pay him back. I had to; I couldn't get out of it now. It was touching really; Bruno was the least able to give me money.

The trip up to Neuilly cost me three francs and I spent another one franc thirty on more coffee when I got to the stop. I gave no thought to how I would get back if I didn't get the job, but I did think it would seem odd to turn up carrying a suitcase, as if I was certain I would be taken on. So I left the case with the café barman and, following his directions, eventually found the address.

Find out more about RedDoor
Press and sign up to our
newsletter to hear about our
latest releases, author events,
exciting **competitions**
and more at

reddoorpress.co.uk

YOU CAN ALSO FOLLOW US:

 @RedDoorBooks

 Facebook.com/RedDoorPress

 @RedDoorBooks